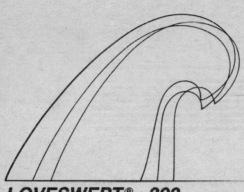

LOVESWEPT® • 392

Janet Evanovich
Smitten

BANTAM BOOKS
NEW YORK • TORONTO • LONDON • SYDNEY • AUCKLAND

SMITTEN

A Bantam Book / April 1990

If you would be interested in receiving protective vinyl
covers for your Loveswept books, please write to this address
for information:

Loveswept
Bantam Books
P.O. Box 985
Hicksville, NY 11802

ISBN 0-553-44024-1

Published simultaneously in the United States and Canada

PRINTED IN THE UNITED STATES OF AMERICA

OPM   0   9   8   7   6   5   4   3   2   1

"You're a mess," Matt said, touching a curl. "You have paint in your hair." He meant to keep it light, but his hand lingered, tracing a line down Lizabeth's cheek, and desire flared between them.

She heard her breath catch in her throat when he stepped closer. She was scared to death he was going to kiss her, and scared to death he wouldn't. They watched each other for a long minute, assessing the attraction. Then Matt dropped his hand and cleared his throat. "You have paint on your cheek."

Lizabeth blinked. "I thought you were going to kiss me."

Matt frowned. "I was thinking about it, but I chickened out."

She could identify with that, she'd backed away from plenty of scary situations. But heck, there was no reason she had to wait for yellow-belly to kiss her. She took a deep breath, grabbed him by the shirt front, and planted a kiss on his perfect lips. But there was no response.

The first kiss was sheer bravado. She took her time on the second one, sliding her hands up his back, enjoying the feel of hard muscle, then tangled her fingers in his blond hair. She didn't seem to notice the rest of the construction crew, but Matt did.

"This is a little embarrassing—" he muttered.

Lizabeth froze. Don't panic, she told herself. You just threw yourself at a man, and he obviously didn't want to catch you. "Okay, I can handle rejection," she said bravely.

"You think I rejected you?" Matt asked. When she nodded, he grinned. Then he pulled her to him with enough force to make her breath catch and claimed her mouth in a kiss that left no doubt about the extent of his desire. . . .

WHAT ARE *LOVESWEPT* ROMANCES?

They are stories of true romance and touching emotion. We believe those two very important ingredients are constants in our highly sensual and very believable stories in the *LOVESWEPT* line. Our goal is to give you, the reader, stories of consistently high quality that may sometimes make you laugh, sometimes make you cry, but are always fresh and creative and contain many delightful surprises within their pages.

Most romance fans read an enormous number of books. Those they truly love, they keep. Others may be traded with friends and soon forgotten. We hope that each *LOVESWEPT* romance will be a treasure—a "keeper." We will always try to publish

LOVE STORIES YOU'LL NEVER FORGET
BY AUTHORS YOU'LL ALWAYS REMEMBER

The Editors

One

When Lizabeth Kane was five years old she wanted to grow up to be a fairy. She wanted skin that was as smooth and white as milkweed silk. And she wanted hair that cascaded halfway down her back in a luxuriant cloud of waves and curls that shone a sunny yellow by day and silver when washed by the light of the moon. She thought she'd wear a buttercup blossom when she needed a hat, and she'd go rafting on curled magnolia leaves.

At five Lizabeth understood that she was a human child and it would take some doing to shrink herself into fairy size, but she had confidence in falling stars and wishbones and birthday candles. She knew that fairies were tiny creatures, no bigger than a man's thumb, but it seemed to her that if a girl could grow up then she could almost as easily grow down. And if she could eventually grow breasts then probably if she tried very hard she could grow wings instead. Almost all fairies had lovely gossamer wings, and Lizabeth wasn't sure how comfortable that would be when she wanted to sleep on her back or lean against the gnarled trunk of an enchanted tree to daydream. She supposed that would be part of the price she would pay for growing up to be a fairy.

In fact, that was about the only price exacted on an adult fairy, because for the most part, fairies did just as they pleased. They weren't stuffed into panty hose and sent off on a bus to earn a living staring at a computer screen. They weren't polite to incompetent employers for the sake of career advancement. And they weren't expected to pre-pare gourmet feasts for boring men who had only one thing on their mind . . . pot roast. Fairies were indulgent, playful creatures, and even though two decades and several years had gone by since Lizabeth first decided to be a fairy, even though Lizabeth Kane now stood five feet six inches tall in her stocking feet, even though she was now thirty-two years old—she still had aspirations of growing up to be a fairy.

She no longer cared about whittling herself down to the average fairy height of five inches, or hav-ing milkweed skin or gobs of fairy hair. Lizabeth Kane wanted the pluck, the joie de vivre, the per-fect thighs of Tinker Bell. Think positive, Lizabeth told herself. If she just put her mind to it she could be plucky, she could have joie de vivre—and two out of three wasn't bad.

She folded the morning paper under her arm and looked at the half-finished house looming in front of her. She had to be positive about getting a job too. She was a single parent now, and if she didn't get a job soon, meeting her mortgage payment was going to be more elusive than obtaining Tinker Bell thighs. She read the crude "Help Wanted" sign stuck into the front yard and took a deep breath. She'd been on fourteen job interviews in the past five days and no one had even given her a second look. She was overeducated. She was undereducated. She was inexperienced. She was unskilled. She was virtually unemployable. Okay, Lizabeth, she said to herself, pulling her shoulders back, this is a new day. This is your last shot. And this is the perfect job. Perfect hours, perfect location, decent wages. Go for it! she told herself.

Matt Hallahan had been looking out of an upstairs window. He'd watched Lizabeth fold her paper and chew on her lower lip while she stared at the house. Not a buyer, he decided. Buyers came in pairs and usually had a real estate agent in tow. This woman looked as if she were peddling vacuum cleaners and he was her first customer. She was nervous, she was anxious—she was cute as a bug. Even from this distance he could see she had big blue eyes, a little nose, and lots of curly brown hair that hung almost to her shoulders. She was small-boned and slim. Not skinny. Her pink T-shirt stretched tight over full breasts and was tucked into a pair of formfitting, faded jeans. He didn't know what she was selling, but he admitted to himself that he'd have a hard time not buying it. She stiffened her spine, pushed her chin forward, and tiptoed through the mud to the front door.

"Yoo-hoo," Lizabeth called. "Anybody home?" She gasped and took a step backward when Matt appeared at the head of the stairs and ambled down to her. He was big. He seemed to fill the whole stairwell. He was half undressed, and he was gorgeous. She felt her heart slam against the back of her rib cage while she made a fast assessment. At least six feet two inches with shoulders like a linebacker and the flat stomach and slim hips of a Chippendales dancer. No shirt, cutoff jeans that rode low, a red heart tattooed on his left forearm. He had muscular legs. Great quads. And he was tan—everywhere. When she finally dragged her eyes up to his face she found he was laughing at her. Smile lines splintered from deep-set blue eyes that were shaded by curly blond eyelashes and a ferocious slash of bushy blond eyebrows. His nose was sunburned and peeling, and his mouth was incredibly tempting.

"Lord, lady," he said, "last time someone looked at me that close was when I thought I had a hernia and the doctor told me to cough."

Lizabeth felt the flush spread from her ears to her cheeks. Get a grip, she told herself. Thirty-two-year-old mothers do not blush. She'd delivered two children, she'd learned to pump gas, she'd seen Tom Cruise, Bruce Willis, and Ted Danson in their underwear. She could handle anything. She ignored his remark and plastered a smile on her face. "I'd like to speak to whoever is in charge of this construction project."

"That's me. Matt Hallahan." He held out his hand.

"Lizabeth Kane." He didn't rub his thumb across

her wrist. He didn't give her an extra squeeze or prolong the contact. He just shook her hand. She liked him for that. And she liked the way his hand felt. Warm and calloused and firm. "I'd like to apply for the job you advertised in the paper."

Matt missed a beat before answering. "I advertised for a carpenter."

"Yup."

His grin widened. Life was full of nice surprises. "You have any experience?"

"Actually, I haven't done much carpentering professionally. But I've hammered a lot of nails into things—you know, hanging pictures—and once I built a dollhouse from scratch, all by myself."

The smile tightened at the corners of his mouth. "That's it?"

"I suppose I was hoping it would be an entry-level position."

"Entry level in the construction business would be laborer."

Lizabeth caught her bottom lip between her teeth. "Oh. Well then, I'd like to apply for a job as a laborer."

"Honey, you're too little to be a laborer. Laborers do a lot of carting around." He squeezed her bicep. "Look at this. Hardly any muscle at all. You probably have one of those motor-driven Hoovers."

Lizabeth narrowed her eyes. She didn't like being called a wimp. "I can do a push-up."

"Only one?"

"One is pretty good. Besides, I've just started on my exercise program. Next week I'll be up to two . . . maybe three."

"Wouldn't you rather be a secretary? You could work in a nice air-conditioned office . . ."

"No," Lizabeth said firmly. "I would not rather be a secretary. To begin with, I can't type. I break out in hives when I sit in front of a computer screen. I can't do *anything*! You know why I can't do anything? Because when I went to college I majored in history. My mother told me to major in math, but did I listen to her? Nooooo. I could have been an accountant. I could have been self-employed. And if that isn't bad enough, I've spent the last ten years of my life reading Little Bear books and baking chocolate-chip cookies." She was pacing, flapping her arms. "Now I need a job, and I can't do anything. If I don't get a job, I can't meet my mortgage payments. My kids will starve. I heard of a woman once who got so desperate she cooked her dog." Lizabeth gave an involuntary shiver.

"You have kids?"

"Two boys. Ten and eight. You see, that's why this job is so perfect for me. I only live about a quarter mile away. I've been watching the new houses going up, and I noticed the carpenters stop work at three-thirty. My kids get out of school at three-thirty. I wouldn't have to put them in day care if I worked here."

He looked at her left hand. No ring. He was doomed. How could he refuse a job to a woman who was about to barbecue Spot to keep her kids from starving?

"I'm much bigger than I look," Lizabeth said. "And besides, that's another thing about the job that's perfect. It would get me into shape. And I would learn things about a house. I need to know about fixing toilets and roofs and getting tiles to stick to floors."

"How soon do you have to know all these things?"

"The sooner the better."

Matt grimaced. "Your roof is leaking? Your toilet has a problem? Your tiles are coming loose?"

"Yes. But it's not as bad as it sounds. I bought this terrific house. It was built at the turn of the century and has gingerbread trim and elaborate cornices and wonderful woodwork, but it's a little run-down . . ."

"You're not talking about that gray Victorian on the corner of Woodward and Gainsborough, are you?"

Lizabeth nodded her head. "That's it. That's my house."

"I always thought that house was haunted. In fact, I thought it was condemned."

"It's not haunted. And it was only condemned because the front porch needed fixing." She paused in her pacing and looked at him. "You don't think it's hopeless, do you?"

He wasn't sure if she was talking about her house or his life after this moment. It didn't matter. The answer would be the same to both questions—yes. But he lied. "No. I think the house has . . . possibilities. It has . . . character."

Lizabeth smiled. She loved her house. It had a few problems, but it was charming and homey and just looking at it made her happy. She'd bought it in January, the day after her divorce had become final. She'd needed to do something positive. Give herself a symbolic fresh start. "Maybe you could come over sometime and take a look at it. You could give me your professional opinion on it. I'm not sure which project I should start first."

His professional opinion was that the house should be burned to the ground. He wasn't able to tell her that, though, because his heart was painfully stuck in his throat. It had happened when she'd smiled. She had the most beautiful, the most radiant smile he'd ever seen. And he'd caused it just by saying her house had character. He wondered if she would smile like that if he kissed her—if he made love to her. He lounged against the unpainted wall, his arms loosely crossed over his bare chest, and he promised himself that someday he'd take Lizabeth Kane to bed, and when she awoke in the morning, she'd open her eyes and see him lying beside her, and she'd smile.

Lizabeth saw his eyes grow soft and sexy and worried that he'd misinterpreted her invitation. She hadn't meant to be so friendly. She didn't want to imply that she'd do *anything* to get the job. It was just that it was difficult for her to be less than exuberant when it came to her house. And in all honesty, she might have gaped at his body a tad too long. "I didn't mean to sound so desperate for the job," she said. "This is my first construction interview, and I think I got carried away. I don't want you to hire me because you feel sorry for me with my leaky roof and two hungry kids. And I don't want you to hire me because . . . well, you know."

He raised his eyebrows in question.

Lizabeth rolled her eyes and made a disgusted sound. She was making a fool of herself. She'd approached him about a job and had ended up telling him her life story, and now she was in the awkward position of establishing sexual boundaries. She'd been separated from her husband for a year and a half and divorced for six months, but she still wasn't especially good at being a sophisticated single. It wasn't a matter of time, she admitted. It was a matter of personality. She was an impulsive, let-it-all-hang-out, emotional dunderhead. "Look," she said flatly, "I'm willing to work hard. I'm smart. I'm dependable. I'm honest." She pulled a folded piece of lined notebook paper from her pocket and handed it to him. "This is my résumé. It's not much, but it has my name and address and phone number, and if you ever need a laborer you can get in touch with me."

Matt unfolded the paper and studied it, trying to keep the grin from creeping across his mouth. "This is a spelling list."

Lizabeth snatched it back and winced as she looked at it. "I took the wrong paper. This is my son's homework assignment."

"Don't worry about it. I don't need a résumé. And it so happens I do need a laborer."

"You're not hiring me out of pity, are you?"

"No, of course not." That was an honest answer, he thought. He was hiring her out of lust. He didn't think she wanted to hear that, so he decided not to elaborate. "You can start tomorrow, if you want. Be here at six o'clock."

She did it! She got the job! If Matt Hallahan hadn't been so overwhelmingly virile she would have kissed him, but she instinctively knew kissing Matt Hallahan would be serious stuff. It would start out as a spontaneous act of happiness and gratitude, and it would end up as pure pleasure. A fairy wouldn't have hesitated for a second, but Lizabeth Kane wasn't a fairy. She was a mother, so she gave herself a mental hug and smiled.

Matt couldn't help smiling back. Her joy was infectious. He stuffed his hands into his pockets to keep from touching her, and wondered what the devil he was going to do with a soft, gullible, 123-pound laborer.

Jason Kane looked at his mother with the sort of cynical excitement peculiar to eight-year-old boys. "Man, this is awesome. My mom, a construction worker. You're gonna bust your buns," he said gleefully. "Those construction workers are tough. They have muscles out to here. They chew tobacco, and they have tattoos. Are you gonna get a tattoo, Mom?"

Lizabeth paused with her knife in the peanut butter jar. "Excuse me? Bust your buns?"

"That's construction-worker talk, Mom. You'd better get used to it."

Ten-year-old Billy was less enthusiastic. "You sure you can handle this, Mom? You're pretty puny. And you're old."

"I'm not *that* old. I'm thirty-two!" She slathered peanut butter on a slice of bread. "I'm going to be fine. I won't be far away, and I'll have a good-paying job. You two can watch television until Aunt Elsie gets here."

Their eyes opened wide. "Aunt Elsie is coming?" they said in unison.

"She's agreed to come stay with us for the summer so you won't be on your own all day."

Jason sprang out of his seat. "Mom, Aunt Elsie is a hundred years old. She talks to pigeons."

"Aunt Elsie isn't a hundred years old," Lizabeth said. She wrapped her peanut butter and jelly sandwich in a plastic bag and dropped it into a brown paper sack, along with a can of root beer and an apple. "Aunt Elsie is seventy-two and she's almost as good as new."

"They keep her locked up in a camp for old people," Billy said.

Lizabeth tossed the rest of her coffee down her throat. "I have to go. I don't want to be late the first day. And it's not a camp. It's a retirement village, and the man at the gate keeps trespassers out. He doesn't keep Aunt Elsie locked in."

Billy and Jason looked at each other as if they didn't believe her.

Lizabeth stood at the front door. "You guys know the rules. Don't open the door to strangers. Call Mrs. Fee next door if there's a problem. My work address and phone number are posted on the bulletin board in the kitchen."

Billy put his arm around his little brother. "Don't worry, Mom. I can handle it."

"Mmmmm." They were great kids, Lizabeth thought, but Jason had his "ice cream for lunch" look. Good thing Elsie said she'd be there by ten. She kissed both boys and locked the door behind her.

The morning air felt cool on her face. Birds sang. Cicadas droned. Harbingers of hot weather, Lizabeth thought, taking a moment to listen to the insects. Bucks County was lovely in the summer. Lush and green, the air fragrant with the smell of flowers, cut grass, and fresh-turned dirt. The land bordering the Delaware River was a flat, rich floodplain, steeped in history, dotted by quaint towns unmarred by shopping centers and suburban sprawl. This was where Lizabeth chose to live. Chase Mills, Pennsylvania. Seven miles from Washington's Crossing and a forty-five-minute drive from downtown Philadelphia.

Lizabeth wore jeans and a yellow T-shirt and she swung her lunch bag as she walked. The smell of coffee percolating in kitchens carried through the open windows. The newspaper boy cut through front yards, slinging his papers onto porches. Lizabeth could hear him marching up Gainsborough Drive. "Thunk," the paper would hit against a front door. A patch of silence and then another "thunk." In new neighborhoods, like the small cul-de-sac Matt was building, there would be the whir of central air conditioners. Lizabeth's street had no whirring sounds. The houses on Lizabeth's street were old, each one unique, built before the age of the subdivision, and they lacked some of the fancier amenities. The sidewalks were cracked and sometimes tilted from tree roots snaking beneath them. Houses sat back from the street, shaded by mature, thickly leaved maples and hundred-year-old oaks. Bicycles waited on wooden porches that wrapped around clapboard houses. It was a family neighborhood that was gently dealing with mid-life crises. A few homes had succumbed to vinyl siding, but as yet no one had installed a hot tub. Dogs ran loose. Lawns were trimmed but were far from manicured. There was too much shade, too many roots, too many tiny feet tramping through yards for perfect lawns. Rosebushes lined driveways and grew along the occasional picket fence.

Lizabeth walked to the end of Gainsborough Drive and turned into the new, blacktopped cul-de-sac that pushed into a small bit of woods. There were three houses under construction. There was room for four more. A plumber's truck was parked in front of the first house, which was a large colonial, almost completed. Two pickups and a jeep were parked farther down the street. A radio blared. Hammers rhythmically slammed into wood and from inside one of the houses a saw whined. Lizabeth could barely hear any of it over the pounding of her heart. She wiped sweaty palms on her jeans and tried to move forward, but her feet refused to budge. She had no business being here! She belonged back home, in her kitchen. Lizabeth, she told herself, you're a liberated woman. There's no reason for you to live your life in a kitchen. Yes there is, she silently wailed, I *like* my kitchen. I feel comfortable there. I know how to use a food processor. I do not know how to use a caulking gun. Okay, bottom line. She didn't get paid for working in her kitchen. But why had she chosen this? What had she been thinking yesterday? The answer was obvious. She was thinking of her kids. She took a deep breath. "Okay. I can do it," she said under her breath. "I'm ready. Come on, feet. Get going."

• • •

Matt's office was in a small corner of the colonial's unfinished basement. It consisted of a desk, a file cabinet, and a telephone. He spent the first hour of each morning on the phone tracking down building inspectors, roofers, landscapers, and carpenters. As Matt finished his first call, Howie White stood at the top of the stairs and yelled down. "Hey, boss, maybe you'd better come take a look at this. There's a lady standing at the end of the street and she's talking to herself. I don't think she's got both oars in the water."

"Is she pretty, about five feet six, with curly brown hair?"

"Yeah."

"Her name's Lizabeth. Go fetch her. Tell her I sent you."

Five minutes later Lizabeth stood in front of the desk. "I was just getting ready to look for you," she said.

"I figured." He cradled the phone to his ear and poured out two cups of coffee. "Howie had other ideas, though. He figured you were waiting to jump in front of a bus."

"I was having trouble with my feet," Lizabeth said. "They were cold."

Matt handed her a cup of coffee. "Here. Maybe this will warm them up. I have to make a few more phone calls and then we can get out of this basement. As you can see, this is a pretty small operation. I have a partner, but he's in the hospital in a body cast."

"How awful. What happened?" Visions of failed building machinery filled her head.

"Fell off his kid's skateboard and broke his hip.

Anyway, we own seven building lots on this cul-de-sac. We've got three houses going up. This one's sold. The other two are spec houses." He saw the question in her eyes. "That means we're building them on speculation. We're using our own money to build and hoping to sell the houses at a good profit when they're done. We subcontract plumbers, carpenters, roofers, drywallers, but we do a lot of the work ourselves."

Lizabeth drank her coffee and watched him. Today he wore a black T-shirt tucked into a pair of faded jeans, and Lizabeth thought he was the most awesome man she'd ever encountered. He was a genetic masterpiece. He was freshly shaven, his blond hair was parted and combed, and his shirt and jeans still held the crease from being laundered and folded. Concessions to civilization, Lizabeth thought. She wasn't about to be fooled by the crease in his jeans. Anyone with eyebrows like that and a tattoo on his arm had to be part barbarian. She guessed at which part, and her conclusion triggered a rush of adrenaline.

"Okay, I'm done." He pushed the phone away and flipped the switch on the answering machine. "I'm going to have you paint trim today." It was the easiest job he could come up with on short notice. She wouldn't have to lift anything heavy, and she wouldn't be near power tools. He handed her a can of white latex enamel. "All you have to do is put a coat of this over the wood that's been primed." He gave her a narrow brush and led the way up the stairs. "You can put your lunch in the refrigerator in the kitchen, and feel free to use the phone to call home if you want to check on your kids."

"Thanks, but they'll be fine. My Aunt Elsie is coming to baby-sit for a while."

Matt nodded. He didn't want to leave her. He wanted to stay and talk to her about her kids, her Aunt Elsie, her sorry house. And he wanted to touch her. He wanted to splay his hand against the small of her back, draw her tight against him, and kiss her for a very long time. He wasn't sure why he found her so desirable. Lately, it seemed the women he met were far less interesting than the houses he built. Lizabeth Kane was the exception. Lizabeth Kane seemed like she would be fun. She reminded him of a kid, waiting in line for her first ride on a roller coaster. She had that frightened look of breathless expectation. He thought about the kiss and decided it might be considered job harassment. He'd been called a lot of things in his thirty-four years. He didn't want to add "sexist pig" to the list. "Well," he said, "if you need me just give a holler." For lack of a better gesture he gave her a light punch in the arm and left her alone with her can of paint.

Two hours later Matt looked in on Lizabeth. She'd made her way up to the second floor, and she was happily singing the theme song from *Snow White.*

"Hi ho, hi ho, it's off to work we go . . ." Lizabeth sang as she swiped at the woodwork on her hands and knees.

"Which one are you?" Matt asked. "Dopey? Doc? Sneezy? Sexy?"

Lizabeth stood and cocked an eyebrow. "There's no dwarf named Sexy."

Matt searched his mind. "Are you sure?"

"Trust me on this."

She had paint on her arms, her jeans, her shoes. It was in her hair, splattered on the front of her shirt, and she had a smudge running the length of her cheek. Matt couldn't keep a grin from surfacing. "You're a mess." He reached out and touched a drooping curl. "You have paint in your hair." He'd meant to keep his touch light, his voice casual and teasing, but his hand lingered. His fingertip traced a line down her temple to just below her ear, and desire flared unexpectedly between them.

Lizabeth heard her own breath catch in her throat when he stepped closer. She was scared to death he was going to kiss her, and scared to death that he wouldn't. They watched each other for a long moment, assessing the attraction.

Matt had always felt fairly competent at second-guessing women—until this moment. He didn't want to make any mistakes with Lizabeth Kane. He didn't want to come on too strong or too fast and frighten her away. And he didn't want to make working conditions awkward. And besides that, she was a mother. He'd never before been involved with a mother. In his eyes motherhood was in the same category as a PhD in physics. It was outside his sphere of knowledge. It was intimidating. And the thought of bedding someone's mother felt a smidgeon irreverent. Not enough to stop him, he thought ruefully. Just enough to slow him down. He considered asking her out, but the words stuck in his throat.

He was standing very close to her with his fingertip barely skimming the smooth, warm line of her jaw. He'd heard the brief intake of breath at his touch and wondered if it was an indication of desire or distress. Perhaps he'd just caught her by surprise. Probably she thought he was a dunce to be standing here with his heart on his sleeve. He dropped his hand and managed a small smile. "You have some paint on your cheek."

Lizabeth blinked at him. "I thought you were going to kiss me."

Matt grimaced. "I was thinking about it, but I chickened out."

She could identify with that. She'd backed away from a lot of frightening situations in the past ten years. Now she was trying to broaden her horizons, get some courage, assert herself. It wasn't easy.

Well, what the heck, Lizabeth thought, this was a new age for women. There was no reason in the world why she had to wait for yellow-belly here to kiss her. There was nothing written in stone that said he had to be the aggressor. She took a deep breath, grabbed him by the shirt front, pulled him to her, and planted a kiss on his perfect lips.

There was no response. Matt Hallahan stood like a wooden Indian with his arms at his sides, his lips slightly parted—in shock, rather than passion—his eyes open wide. Lizabeth checked him to make sure he wasn't hyperventilating and kissed him again. The first kiss had been sheer bravado. The second was much more indulgent. Lizabeth took her time on the second kiss. She slid her hands up the front of his shirt, enjoying the feel of hard muscle, until the tips of her fingers tangled in his blond hair and her thumbs brushed along the lobes of his ears. She kissed him lightly, tentatively. She parted her lips and kissed him again with more insistence.

Matt's reaction was guarded. There were at least twenty men wandering around on the job site with easy access to the colonial. Howie was downstairs, installing a chair rail in the dining room, and Zito was hanging cabinets in the kitchen. Men's bodies weren't designed to conceal emotion, Matt acknowledged. Any second now he was going to do his Hulk imitation—the part where the Hulk's body swells up so big it rips right out of its clothes. This didn't seem like a good time for that to happen, so he placed his hands on Lizabeth's waist and gently pushed her away. "This is a little embarrassing . . ."

Lizabeth snapped her eyes open, made a small, strangled sound in her throat, and smoothed her moist hands on the front of her jeans. Don't panic, she told herself. You just threw yourself at a man who obviously didn't want to catch you. It's not the end of the world. You read the signs wrong. No big deal. In twenty or thirty years, you'll get over it. "Well, I guess that didn't work out, huh? It's okay; I mean, I can handle rejection."

"You think I rejected you?"

"I'm sort of new at this. I don't date much. In fact, I don't date at all. And the problem is I want to be a fairy . . ."

He pulled her to him with enough force to make

her breath catch in her throat, and before she could recover, his mouth claimed hers in a kiss that left no doubt about the extent of his desire. Raw passion, hot and hard, arrowed into her as his tongue swept hers and his hands crushed her against him.

He broke from the kiss and held her at arm's length, taking a moment to let his pulse rate slow. "Would you like me to spell it out?"

"Nope. Not necessary. I think I've got it put together." She licked lips that felt scorched and swollen. "Maybe it would be a good idea to talk about this later . . . when my ears stop ringing."

Two

Billy and Jason Kane had their noses pressed to the living room window when Elsie pulled up in her powder-blue '57 Cadillac.

"Holy cow," Jason said, "did you ever see a car like that? It's bigger than our garage. It's awesome."

Billy rolled his eyes back in his head. "Man, this is gonna be embarrassing."

Elsie parked in the driveway and shook her head at the house. Lizabeth was her favorite niece. She was bright and honest and tenderhearted to a fault. She was not especially practical, though. As a little girl she'd never allowed reality to get in the way of her imagination. And from the looks of her house, she hadn't changed much. The gray paint was peeling down to bare wood, and shutters hung at odd angles. One had fallen off completely and lay on the ground. Elsie looked up to the eaves, half expecting to see bats roosting. While she was studying the eaves, a squirrel jumped from a three-story oak tree onto the shake roof. Several pieces of the roof broke loose and came skittering down, crashing onto the ground. The squirrel slid along with the rotted cedar shakes until it reached the galvanized gutter, where it clung for dear life. The gutter broke loose from its moorings and swung free at one end, hurtling the squirrel into space for about twenty feet before it safely landed in an overgrown lilac bush. "Next time stay off of the roof," Elsie shouted at the squirrel. "Damn pea-brained rodent." She wrestled two huge suitcases out of the Caddy's backseat and headed for the front door.

"This is probably how you feel when you're in the water and you see Jaws coming," Jason said.

Billy opened the door and Elsie staggered in with the suitcases.

"Just because I'm having a time with these suitcases, don't for a minute think I'm some weak old lady," Elsie said.

Billy shook his head vigorously. "No ma'am. I didn't think that."

"And don't think I'm boring, either. I ever tell you about the time I caught a dope dealer practically single-handedly? Smacked right into him with that big old Cadillac. That was before I was married to Gus." She gave the living room a cursory glance and moved into the kitchen. "Too bad you kids never got to meet Gus. We were only married for two months when he had a heart attack." She opened the refrigerator and took stock. "You kids have lunch yet?"

"No," Jason said. "And I'm allergic to liver. It makes me throw up."

"Yeah," Elsie said, "I know what you mean. I was thinking more in the way of ice cream. How about we have ice cream for lunch." She set a half-gallon of chocolate ice cream on the table and found three spoons. "So what do you guys do for fun around here? You ever play bingo?"

Lizabeth watched Matt wipe the paint from the rim of the half-filled can and thump the lid secure with a hammer. She'd graduated magna cum laude from Amherst, but at the advanced age of thirty-two she didn't know the proper way to close up a can of paint. It was embarrassing. She hated being a helpless female.

Matt slid the can into a corner and turned to Lizabeth. "Now you know just about everything there is to know about painting."

She shook her head. "I don't know how to paint with a roller. After I learn how to use a roller I'm going to paint my living room."

"You don't need to learn how to paint with a roller. You go to a hardware store, and they'll give you a starter kit. It's easy." He saw the doubt on her face. "Didn't you ever help your husband paint?"

Lizabeth almost burst out laughing at the thought of Paul Kane with a paintbrush in his hand. "My husband never painted. He hired people to paint."

"How about your dad? Didn't he ever paint anything?"

"My father is Malcolm Slye. If you were from Virginia you'd know that name. He's a third-generation tobacco baron, and he was smart enough to diversify. He works very hard, but he doesn't paint."

"That's a shame," Matt said. "There's a lot of satisfaction to painting. One minute you've got a dirty, dreary wall and the next thing you know it's fresh and clean. Instant gratification." He unplugged the coffeepot and shut the basement lights off. "So you were the poor little rich girl, huh?"

"No. I was the rich little rich girl. I had a terrific childhood. I just never learned to paint."

"Uh-huh. What happened to Mister Wonderful, the guy who hired painters."

"You mean my ex-husband?" Her eyes narrowed slightly and the line of her mouth tightened. "It turned out we had different expectations about marriage. Paul expected me to close my eyes to constant indiscretions, and I expected him to be faithful to me."

"I'm sorry."

Lizabeth waved it away. "Actually, I could have lived with that. What finally drove me out of the marriage was when he insisted that the boys go to boarding school. Paul had political ambitions. He wanted me to be a perfect hostess. He found the children to be a burden."

"I don't think I like this guy."

"He was very charming," Lizabeth said. "But he was a jerk."

Matt studied her. She was okay. Really okay. She had strength. He grabbed her hand and led her up the stairs. "C'mon, I'm going to give you a ride home. And if you want I'll take a look at your house."

"I should warn you about my Aunt Elsie first," Lizabeth said. "Aunt Elsie is from my mother's side of the family. She's a little outspoken."

"I can handle it. I'm pretty brave when it comes to old ladies."

"You've never met an old lady like Aunt Elsie."

Matt could hear the affection in her voice. "She must be something special."

"She's . . . unique."

Ten minutes later they drove down Gainsborough and Matt parked his 4×4 Ford pickup in front of Lizabeth's house. The yard was tidy, and someone had planted clusters of flowers along the front porch, but the house itself was even worse than he'd remembered. His attention was distracted by the car in the driveway. "My God, what is that?"

"That's Elsie's car. If you see her on the road give her a wide berth. She didn't learn to drive until last year, and she doesn't have it perfected yet."

A small gray cat sat on the porch watching their approach.

"This is Bob the Cat. He adopted us about a week ago." She reached down and scratched the kitten's neck. The front door opened and two small boys tumbled out.

"Mom! We're had the most awesome day," Jason said. "Aunt Elsie's here. She took us for a ride in her car. It gets six miles to a gallon of gas. It's radical."

Billy was radiant. "She ran over the summer-school crossing guard's hat and got a ticket. And then she clipped a parking meter downtown. The meter had a big dent in it, but nothing happened to her car. Mom, that car is like a *tank*!"

"I heard that," Elsie said. "It wasn't my fault I ran over that policewoman's hat. She practically threw it in the middle of the road, right in front of my car."

"Yeah," Billy said, "she got real flustered when she saw us barreling down on her in the Cadillac. She tried to jump out of the way and her hat flew off."

Lizabeth winced. "Elsie, you weren't speeding with the boys in the car, were you?"

"I don't think so, but sometimes my foot sticks on the floor mat . . ."

Billy rolled his eyes. "She wasn't speeding. She was barely moving. We never went over twenty-five. It was that she was driving down the middle of the road."

"It's that dang big car," Elsie said. "It don't fit in one lane. When I get some money I'm going to get myself one of them nice little Japanese cars." She noticed Matt standing to one side of the family group. "Who's this?"

"This is my boss, Matt Hallahan," Lizabeth said. "He's come over to take a look at the house for me. Matt, this is my aunt, Elsie Hawkins."

Elsie Hawkins had tightly curled steel-gray hair, sharp blue eyes, and an uncompromising mouth. She was dressed in support hose, tennis shoes, and a tailored blue shirtwaist dress that came to just below her knees. Matt thought she looked like she could wrestle alligators and win.

Lizabeth affectionately ruffled Jason's hair. "And these are my sons, Jason and Billy."

Both boys had brown hair that had recently been cut. They were dressed in shorts and polo shirts and had skinned knees and quick smiles.

"Wow, he's got a tattoo," Jason said. "Neat!"

Elsie looked at the tattoo. "What's that funny writing on it?"

Matt felt his cheeks flush. He had mixed feelings about his tattoo. "It's Chinese. I joined the Navy right out of high school. We made a port call in Taiwan, and I got drunk and ended up with this tattoo."

"Pretty fancy," Elsie said. "What do those Chinese squiggles mean?"

"Uh . . ." He shifted from one foot to the other. "It's sort of a rhyme. It has to do with . . . sexual relations with a duck."

Elsie clamped her hand over her mouth to keep from giggling. "That's terrible," she said.

"I know what it is!" Jason said. "I heard it on cable television. It's . . ."

"Jason Kane!" Lizabeth said. "Don't you have a football to throw around?"

"Ferguson ate it."

"Ferguson's our dog," Lizabeth explained to Matt. "He eats things."

Matt grinned. The place was a loony bin. He loved it.

Lizabeth made an expansive gesture with her arms. "Well, what do you think of the house?"

He looked around critically. Even if he helped her, he doubted she could afford to do all the necessary work. His guess was she was trying to make it on her own, without her father's or her husband's money, and she was having a tough time of it. "Needs a little paint," he volunteered. "Maybe a few new shakes for the roof."

Elsie looked at him sideways. "Cut the baloney. What do you think it really needs?"

"A lot of paint. It has to be scraped and primed and then painted. It needs an entire new roof, new aluminum gutters, and all of the shutters need to be rehung."

"So, you're in the construction business," Elsie said. "I suppose you got ladders and paint scrapers and such. Why don't you stay for supper. We're having meat loaf."

Lizabeth groaned. "Aunt Elsie, that's not very subtle."

"I'm an old lady. I don't have to be subtle."

Matt grinned. "Meat loaf sounds great."

Elsie looked him over. "You a bachelor?"

"Yup."

"You could do worse," she said to Lizabeth.

Lizabeth glared a warning at Elsie. "He's my *boss!*"

"He make a pass at you yet?"

Lizabeth felt her ears burning.

"I knew it," Elsie said, turning back to the house. "Supper'll be ready at five-thirty."

An hour later Matt sat on the porch steps and reviewed his findings with Lizabeth. "The toilets are easy and inexpensive to fix. You can do them right away. I have some rollers and brushes you can borrow, and for a relatively small amount of money you can paint the interior. You can do it one room at a time, if you want. The floors are going to need a professional. You have a new water heater and the furnace doesn't look half bad. That's on the plus side."

"Someday, this house is going to be beautiful," Lizabeth said. "I'm going to paint it yellow with white trim, and I'm going to plant flowers everywhere."

Matt leaned against the railing and closed his eyes. He was jealous of her, he realized. She had two kids and a wacky aunt, a dog, a cat, a house she loved. She had a future that was filled to the brim with life. Somehow, he hadn't fashioned that for himself. He lived in a rented town house, all alone. And he built houses for other people. It had always been enough, but right now it seemed depressingly deficient. "Lizabeth, your house is beautiful *now*. It will always be beautiful. It doesn't have anything to do with paint or plumbing or petunias. Your house is beautiful because you're beautiful."

It was a full minute before she could respond. No one had ever said anything like that to her before. It was the most perfect compliment she could imagine. Her eyes filled with tears, and she bit into her lower lip. "Thank you."

"Oh damn, you're not going to cry, are you?"

"I'm very emotional. It's one of my faults."

It was the sort of fault he could get used to, he thought. You would always know where you stood with her. She was guileless.

Jason ran across the lawn after a softball. He swept it up and threw it to his brother. "You want to play with us?" he asked Matt. "We need a pitcher."

"Do I get to bat?"

"Sure, you can be up first, but you'll never get anything off of Billy. He stinks as a pitcher."

Matt took the bat and knocked it against his rubber-soled boots a couple of times. He shuffled his feet and practiced his batter's stance. He looked Billy in the eye and set himself back for the pitch. "Okay, Billy Kane, give me your best shot," he said.

Billy slow-pitched him an underhand bloop. Matt smiled and swung, enjoying the feel of connecting with the ball. It was a perfect line drive, fast and hard, and zoomed straight as an arrow to Elsie's Cadillac, where it shattered the passenger-side window.

There was a full minute of silence.

"You're a dead man," Billy said. "She's gonna kill you."

"Quick, get the baseball," Jason said. "We'll tell her a meteor did it."

The screen door squeaked on its rusty hinges and Elsie stepped out onto the porch. "What was that crash?" There was an audible gasp when she saw her car, and then her false teeth came together with a sharp "click." She surveyed the group of bystanders with steely eyes and with her mouth drawn into a tight little line. Her eyes locked in on Matt, standing flat-footed, grinning his most endearing, sheepish grin, still holding the bat.

"Got good stuff on the ball?" she asked him.

"He's going to help us fix the toilets," Lizabeth said.

Elsie didn't blink. "The toilets, huh?"

"She doesn't look impressed," Matt whispered

to Lizabeth. "Maybe we should up the ante. Tell her I'm going to paint the living room. Tell her I'll put a new floor in the bathroom."

"That isn't necessary," Lizabeth said. "It was an accident."

"I know that, and you know that, but Elsie looks like she's contemplating death by meat loaf." He looked over Lizabeth's shoulder at Elsie. "New bathroom floors," he called to her. "Ceramic tile."

That caught Elsie's attention. "Ceramic tile? Does that include new grout around the tub?"

Matt leaned into Lizabeth and murmured into her hair. "Everybody has his price."

The contact sent a rush of excitement skimming along Lizabeth's spine. She glanced at Matt from the corner of her eye. "Really? What's your price?"

"What do you want to buy?"

"What would you be willing to sell?"

The question hung in the air. He didn't know what he wanted to sell. He was afraid it might be everything. His heart, his soul, his chromosomes. He suspected that he offered to tile the bathroom not because he was afraid of Elsie, but because he wanted to impress Lizabeth. More than that, he wanted to do something nice for her. And he wanted to do something nice for the house. Now that he'd had a chance to see it up close, he realized it had wonderful potential. The basic structure was sound despite years of neglect. It was well laid out and had nice detail. Most important, it was the sort of house that grew on you. It had character. Just like Lizabeth.

When he didn't answer immediately Lizabeth's

mouth curved into a grim smile. "Pretty scary question, huh?"

"The question's okay. It's the answer that's got me shaking in my boots."

Two days later Lizabeth looked at the can of paint Matt had set out for her and felt her temper kick in. "I've been on this job for three days and all I've done is paint trim. I'll admit I'm not too bright about construction work, but I'm smart enough to realize that trim does not ordinarily get four coats of paint."

Matt sighed. He didn't know what to do with her. He'd never had a woman on the job site before. Equal rights was fine in theory, but he didn't know how to go about putting it to work. He had some old-fashioned ideas about women. His natural instinct was to protect and pamper. Asking a woman to clean half a ton of construction debris from a basement made him feel like a brute. And to make matters even more complicated, he was in love. Flat out in love with Lizabeth Kane. Every day his feelings for her grew stronger. It had his stomach tied in knots. He'd asked her out, but she'd turned him down. Probably a weekend in Paris hadn't been a good choice for a first date. He'd gotten carried away, he admitted.

"I want to be treated like any trainee. I want to learn how to do carpenter things," Lizabeth said. "I've been watching the carpenters work on House Three, and most of what they're doing seems pretty straightforward."

"Lizabeth, it's ninety degrees outside, and it's only eight o'clock in the morning."

She crossed her arms over her chest and glared at him.

Matt made a frustrated gesture and kicked the can of paint into a corner. "You win. But you have to work with me. I want you where I can keep an eye on you."

"What kind of an attitude is that?"

"It's the best attitude I can manage right now."

Four hours later Lizabeth pushed her damp hair from her forehead and readjusted the baseball hat Matt had given her. She hadn't been more than three steps away from Matt all morning, hammering one nail for his twenty, and she was sure he was slowing his pace so he wouldn't embarrass her. He'd slathered suntan lotion on her fried neck, bandaged the bleeding blisters on her hands, and kicked a carpenter off the project for unnecessary cussing. He was driving her crazy.

He looked up when she paused in her hammering, and he smiled at her. "Want a soda?"

One more soda and she was sure she'd float away. He'd been pouring liquid into her since ten o'clock. Undoubtedly he knew what he was doing, but she couldn't take any more. "We have to talk."

Thank goodness. He didn't think he could endure another half hour of watching her work. She seemed so frail, with her curly hair tucked under the baseball cap and her yellow T-shirt clinging to her slim frame. Every time she picked up her hammer he felt his stomach tighten. He wanted to whisk her away to a cool restaurant. Get her all dressed up in something pretty and feed her strawberries dipped in chocolate. "We could take an early lunch break and talk in the shade, under the trees," he suggested hopefully.

"I don't want to take an early lunch break. I want to work like the rest of the men. I just don't want to work with *you*."

"Want to run that by me again?"

"You're overprotective. It's sweet of you to want to take care of me, but I need to stand on my own." She began to hammer while she talked. "I want to be accepted as an equal out here. That's never going to happen if you keep hovering over me like a mother hen."

He had a news flash for her. She was never going to be an equal. She was going to be the boss's wife. Equal that! "This is just your first day as a carpenter. You don't know anything."

"I know lots of things. I know how to hammer a nail. I can't hammer nails as fast as you can, but I can hammer them just as well. Look at this one. It's perfect."

Matt looked at the nail and agreed it was pretty good. "Okay, so you can hammer a nail, but you have no common sense. You let yourself get sunburned and blistered. And you try to carry things that are too heavy for you."

He was right. She'd been stupid. "I'll be better. I'll keep my hat on, and I'll wear gloves."

"What about the heavy stuff?"

"You'll have to settle for two out of three. I want to pull my weight."

Matt pressed his lips together. Damn stubborn female. She had him. There was no way he'd ever fire her as long as she wanted the job. And there was no way he could force her to obey his every command. He couldn't exactly duke it out with her if they had a disagreement. She'd never go out with him then. He took a deep breath and studied the toe of his work boot while he got his temper under control. "If you want to continue to work here you're going to have to work with me." He saw her nose belligerently tip up a fraction of an inch and he held up his hands. "However, I'll try to be less of a mother hen."

"I suppose that's an okay compromise." The truth is, she enjoyed being next to him. The shivery excitement was always there, but running parallel to that was a comfortable rapport. Matt Hallahan felt like a friend. Despite his tattoo, he felt like someone she'd known and liked for a very long time. And as long as she was being honest with herself, she had to admit that a part of her enjoyed being clucked over. It had been a lot of years since anyone had regarded her as fragile, probably because she wasn't, and while she couldn't let it interfere with learning her job, she secretly treasured the attention.

She was working on the second deck of the house, laying four-by-eight sections of three-quarter tongue-and-groove plywood. She stuck a nail into the wood and whacked it three times, driving it home. She moved over six inches and set another nail. She was beginning to understand why Matt liked building houses. Every hour you could stand back, look at your progress and know you were making something that would last a long, long time. Children would grow up in the house, they'd leave for college, get married, and return with children of their own—and still the house would remain. It was important that the house be built correctly, she decided. It wasn't just a matter of safety. It had to do with pride and creativity and immortality.

She stood up, took a step backward to admire her handiwork, and fell into the open stairwell. Benny Newfarmer, all two hundred and fifty-four pounds of him, was there to break her fall. He caught her square in the chest and crashed to the floor with a thud that carried the length of the cul-de-sac. Lizabeth sprawled across Newfarmer, stunned by the impact, and then rolled off his huge belly as if it were a giant beachball. "Sorry," she said to him. "Are you all right?"

Newfarmer stared unblinking into space, his breath coming in short gasps.

Bucky Moyer ambled over. "Cripes," he said, "I've never seen him flat on his back like this. He looks like a beached whale."

Lizabeth nervously cracked her knuckles. "Why isn't he saying anything? Why isn't he getting up? Maybe we should call an ambulance."

Bucky grinned. "Nah, he's okay. You just caught him by surprise. He's not used to women jumping on his body like that."

"Yeah, I'm okay," Newfarmer said, struggling to get up. "You just took me by surprise."

Lizabeth glanced over at Matt. He had his hands on his hips and his face looked as if it had been chiseled in granite. It was the sort of steely-eyed, hard-jawed look you get when you grit your teeth for a long time. She grimaced. "Are you mad at me?"

He unclenched his teeth and expelled a long breath. "No, I'm not mad at you. I'm just glad you didn't kill him. It would take a forklift to get him out of here." He unbuckled his carpenter's belt. "Lunch, everyone."

Matt sat back and waited until the men had dispersed. When he was alone with Lizabeth, he stared at her for a long time before speaking. He was torn between wanting to take her in his arms and hold her close, and wanting to shake her until her teeth rattled. "Lizabeth . . ." He was at a loss for words. What the hell was he supposed to say to her? He'd known her less than a week, and his heart had stopped when he saw her disappear down the stairwell. "Lizabeth, you really scared me." He gave a frustrated shake of his head, because what he'd said was so inadequate. If there had been more privacy he would have liked to make love to her. It was desire born of caring rather than passion. He wanted to join with her, share every intimacy, give her more pleasure than she'd ever imagined, let her see how precious she'd become to him. He pulled her to him and took her face in his hands while he slowly lowered his mouth to hers. He kissed her with infinite tenderness, slowly deepening the kiss while his hands roamed along her back, pressing her closer, needing to feel her soft warmth, needing to be reassured that she was all right . . . that she was his, at least for the moment.

Lizabeth tilted her head back so she could look at him. "That felt like a serious kiss."

"Mmmm. I'm having some pretty serious thoughts."

"I don't know if I'm ready for serious thoughts."

The pain went straight to his heart. He clapped a hand to his chest and grunted. "Boy, that hurts. The first time I have long-term plans for a relationship and look where it gets me. Heartbreak City."

He was a flirt, Lizabeth decided. The nicest man she'd ever met, and also the most outrageous. Long-term plans probably meant an hour and a half. She thought about his offer to take her to Paris and smiled, wondering what he would have done if she'd accepted.

"Sorry, I never get serious in the first four days."

"I suppose you're right," he admitted. "Four days isn't a lot of time. How long do you think it will take?"

"To get serious?" Lizabeth smiled. "I don't know. I don't mean to be insulting, but it's not high on my list of priorities. I have to find myself."

"I didn't know you were lost. Maybe you've been looking in the wrong places."

"Easy for you to joke about it," Lizabeth said. "You have a secure personality. You didn't grow up as 'Mac Slye's Kid.' And you didn't spend ten years as Paul Kane's wife and Jason and Billy Kane's mother. I used to buy T-shirts with my name written on them, hoping once in a while people would call me Lizabeth."

"You're exaggerating."

"Not by very much. I liked being a wife and mother, but when I got out on my own I realized my image had been much too closely tied to others."

"Seems to me you have a good grip on your image."

She studied his face, decided he meant it, and felt a rush of happiness. There were times, toward the end of her marriage, when she wasn't sure if there was any Lizabeth left at all. It was wonderful to know she'd survived.

"Well, we could be friends for a while," she said. "We could see how it turns out."

Three

"Mom's home!" Jason yelled, looking out the front window. "She's with Mr. Hallahan, and he's helping her up the sidewalk."

"What's the matter with her?" Elsie called from the kitchen. "Why does she need help?"

"I dunno. She's all wet, and she's walking funny."

Elsie went to the door and watched her niece slowly make her way up the porch stairs. "Now what?"

Matt tried to look concerned, but his mouth kept twitching with laughter. "She lost her balance and fell into a freshly poured cement driveway. We had to hose her down before the cement set, but there were a few places we missed . . . like her shoes and her underwear."

"I didn't lose my balance," Lizabeth snapped. "I was signing my initials in the wet cement and one of *your* workmen snuck up behind me and got fresh."

Elsie shook her finger at her niece. "I told you, you gotta be careful about bending over when you're around them construction workers."

Lizabeth swiped at the wet hair plastered to her face. "I don't want to talk about it."

Elsie looked at Matt. "Well? Is that the whole story? How come she lost her balance?"

"She lost her balance when she punched him in the nose," Matt said, smiling broadly. It had been a terrific punch. Square on the snoot. He couldn't have done it better himself.

"No kidding?" Elsie was obviously pleased. "That comes from her mother's side of the family. We're a feisty bunch. So how about this guy's nose—did she flatten it?"

"Wasn't exactly flattened," Matt said, "but it was definitely broken."

"Wow," Jason said, "that's so cool. Wait'll I tell the guys. My mom broke someone's nose!"

"It was an accident!" Lizabeth said. "I reacted without thinking, and his nose got in the way. Now if you'll all excuse me I'm going to take a shower. If I'm not out of the shower in half an hour send up a chisel. And don't you dare invite Matt to supper. He smirked at me all the way home."

"She don't mean it," Elsie said to Matt. "We're having pot roast. We'll eat at six."

Matt stuffed his hands in his pockets and rocked back on his heels. "Sounds good to me. I'll pull the tile up in the downstairs bathroom while I wait. Tomorrow's Saturday. I'll come first thing in the morning and put down a new subfloor."

Lizabeth kicked her clothes into a corner of the bathroom and dragged herself into the shower. Laying plywood was a lot more tiring than painting trim. Chances were, if she hadn't been so tired, she wouldn't have fallen into the cement, she decided. If she hadn't been so tired, she would have sensed Oliver Roth sneaking up behind her. And if she hadn't been so tired, she might have had more patience with Roth's groping. She lathered up and watched the last vestiges of cement sluice down the drain. Thank heaven it hadn't hardened on her. She washed her hair and winced when the water beat against the back of her neck. She was sunburned. Occupational hazard, she told herself, wondering about the statistics on skin cancer for construction workers. The statistics probably weren't good. On the other hand, after another week of pounding nails she'd be so physically fit she'd be able to forget about cardiovascular disease. And there were other things she was learning. Elsie was wrong about carpenters. Most of the men were extremely courteous to her, going out of their way to make her feel comfortable. She shut the water off, wrapped a towel around her head, shrugged into her threadbare terry-cloth robe, and stumbled into her bedroom. She flopped facedown onto the bed and instantly fell asleep.

At six, Jason shook Lizabeth awake. "Mom, it's time for supper. You better hurry up."

Lizabeth opened her eyes halfway and looked drowsily at her youngest son. "Huh?"

He put his face down next to hers, nose to nose, and shouted. "It's time for supper!"

"Gotcha," Lizabeth said. "I'm moving."

"You better move fast. Aunt Elsie doesn't like people being late for supper. She'll whack you one with her wooden spoon. She'll make you eat the stalks on the broccoli." He backed off and ran out of the room. "I'll meetcha down there."

Lizabeth pulled a faded T-shirt over her head, stepped into a pair of old running shorts, and combed her fingers through her hair. She was doing her best to hurry, but her muscles weren't cooperating. Everything ached. Matt had been right. She was a wimp. She was thirty-two years old, and she was falling apart at the seams. She took the stairs one step at a time, mumbling as she went. She stopped grumbling when she saw Matt watching her. "Oh jeez, what are you doing here?"

"Elsie invited me for supper."

"What a nice surprise." About as nice as bubonic plague. She could barely move without screaming in pain, her hair looked like World War III, and she wasn't wearing a bra. As she descended the stairs, she decided it was the last fact that caused his look of rapt fascination.

"You seem kinda tuckered out."

"I'm fine," she said, shuffling past him. "I'm not at all tired. And I'm not the least bit sore."

"Guess you're tougher than I thought."

Jason took a scoop of mashed potatoes. "Good thing you're not tired. Matt said he'd play soccer with us after supper, and you could play too."

Lizabeth noticed it was no longer "Mr. Hallahan." She supposed that was okay. Matt didn't seem to mind the familiarity, and the boys needed to have male friends. She would have preferred someone without a tattoo advocating sex with the animal kingdom, but she wasn't in the mood to quibble. She stared at her fork, wondering if she had the strength to pick it up. "Soccer? That sounds like fun," she said absently. "I could use some exercise." She could use some exercise in the year 2000. Anything before that was going to be a major imposition. Not to worry, she thought. Soccer was at least a half hour away. Right now she had more immediate problems. She needed to figure out a way to eat her meat. Cutting and chewing seemed like insurmountable obstacles.

"Something wrong with the meat?" Elsie asked Lizabeth. "You keep staring at it."

"It's fine, but I'm thinking of becoming a vegetarian. I'm worried about my cholesterol."

"Don't be a ninny," Elsie said. "You're nothing but skin and bones, and you have bags under your eyes. You need meat. How do you think I've kept my looks all these years? I eat right. Except for that time when I tried living in the old people's home. Worst food I've ever seen. Everything got squeezed through a strainer."

"Yuck!" Jason said. "Like baby food." He accidentally tipped over his milk, and it spread, like a flash flood, across the table.

Elsie jumped to her feet and ran for a kitchen towel. Lizabeth mopped up milk with her napkin. And Ferguson seized upon the opportunity to run off with the remainder of the pot roast.

"Ferguson's got the pot roast!" Billy shouted. He reached out for the dog, caught his elbow on the gravy boat, and the gravy boat slid into Matt's plate and smashed, dumping a cup and a half of semi-congealed gravy into Matt's lap.

"Oh, gross," Jason said. "One time Ferguson got sick and made a mess on the rug and it looked just like that."

Elsie watched the pot roast disappear around the corner. "There goes tomorrow's lunch," she said. "Damned if you don't have to be on your toes in this house."

"I guess we should postpone the soccer game until tomorrow," Matt said. "If I play soccer in these clothes, I'll have every dog in the neighborhood following me."

Lizabeth leaned back in her chair and managed a weak smile. She was saved. God bless Ferguson.

There were four bedrooms on the top floor of the old Victorian. Lizabeth had chosen a back bedroom for herself and had meagerly furnished it with a double bed and a secondhand oak dresser. One window looked out at the side yard, the view partially obscured by a mature stand of Douglas fir trees that served as a privacy fence. The other window in Lizabeth's room overlooked the backyard, which was, for the most part, packed dirt. Ferguson had littered the yard with punctured footballs, soccer balls, half-chewed baseballs, and a few mangled shoes. A redwood picnic table and two benches had been left by the previous owner.

The table was seldom used for picnics, since Lizabeth didn't have a grill. Instead, it served as the collection point for half-filled jars of soap bubbles, used boxes of crayons, a handful of Matchbox cars, empty juice glasses, plastic water pistols, and whatever other flotsam accumulated from two boys at play. Since the yard was dominated by several large trees, it was continuously cast in shade. By moonlight the yard seemed solemn and spooky, and usually only Bob the Cat ventured into its black shadows.

This evening a human form picked its way around the footballs, soccer balls, and baseballs. He cursed when he stepped on a shoe and stood still for a minute to get his bearings. He moved back a few feet and took a handful of small stones from his coat pocket.

As Lizabeth pulled herself up from the drowse of sleep, she thought it must be sleeting. She lay absolutely still, very quietly listening to the "tik tik tik" of something hitting against her windowpane, and realized, as she became more awake, that it was summer and sleet wasn't possible. It almost sounded as if someone was throwing stones at her window! There was a brief stab of alarm and then she relaxed. Matt. The thought brought a smile to her lips. Poor guy was really smitten with her. Another stone pinged on the glass and Lizabeth swung her legs over the side of the bed. It was two in the morning, and obviously Matt hadn't been able to sleep. She imagined him thrashing around in his bed, feverish with pent-up passion. And now he was here! What was she supposed to do with him? She could hardly invite him up to her bedroom. Maybe he would want to take her back to his apartment. Maybe he wouldn't be able to wait that long. Maybe he'd drag her off into the bushes or lay her out on the picnic table. She hated to admit it, but the picnic table sounded incredibly erotic. She rolled her eyes in the dark bedroom and groaned. What was wrong with her? She was a mother, and mothers didn't go around rutting on picnic tables. Lord, what would her children think? What about Elsie? Lizabeth, she told herself, you're getting weird. That's what happens when you've had a whole lifetime of sexual deprivation. Lizabeth pulled the curtain aside and squinted into the darkness. "Anybody out there?" she called.

There was the distinct rustle of clothing in the darkness below her. A flashlight clicked on and Lizabeth was temporarily blinded as the light played across her face. The intruder held the flashlight aloft, redirecting the beam onto himself, and Lizabeth was treated to a solid minute of full frontal male nudity. The man was wearing a paper-bag mask, a striped tie, and docksiders. "Matt?" Lizabeth whispered. No, of course not. Matt was blond. Then again, blonds might not be blond all over. She stifled a hysterical giggle and dialed the police.

Ten minutes later a black-and-white cruiser pulled up to the house and two policemen met Lizabeth at the door. The taller of the two men looked Lizabeth over. "You the lady who saw the flasher? Can you give us a description?"

"He was pretty ordinary. Not too fat. Not too thin. Average height. I didn't get to see his face, but I'd guess he was in his twenties or early thirties. No chest hair . . ."

Elsie stomped down the stairs in her robe and nightgown. "What's going on here?"

"I thought I was hearing sleet," Lizabeth said, "but it was actually a flasher throwing stones at my window."

Elsie's eyes got wide. "You mean he stood there with no clothes on? Buck naked?"

"He was wearing a tie," Lizabeth said. "And shoes."

"Shoot. I always miss the good stuff," Elsie said. "It isn't fair. I never get to see any naked men."

"This is my Aunt Elsie," Lizabeth explained to the policemen. "She's spending the summer with me."

"Maybe he'll come back," the cop said to Elsie. "You might get another crack at it."

The possibility of that happening made Lizabeth uncomfortable. She didn't like having a naked man skulking around in her yard. "You don't really think he'll come back, do you? Maybe you should stake out my house."

"We don't usually stake out for flashers. If he threatened you, or if there was indication of violence . . ."

Lizabeth shook her head. "No. He just stood there."

Matt rang the doorbell again and looked at his watch. Seven-thirty. The curtains were still drawn and there was no sign of life in Lizabeth's house. It was hard to believe they weren't up yet. Seven-thirty seemed like the middle of the afternoon when you were used to getting up at five every day. He set the bag of doughnuts and the gallon of paint on the porch and walked around the house. Lizabeth's bedroom was in the back. "Lizabeth!" he called in an exaggerated whisper. He cupped his hands to his mouth and called again. There was no response. Her curtain remained closed. He gathered a few stones and tossed them one by one at her window.

Lizabeth woke up with a start. A stone pinged against her windowpane, and her heart jumped to her throat. He was back! She reached for the phone beside her bed and dialed the police, then waited, like a frightened fugitive, while the stones continued to tap on the glass. Five minutes passed on her digital clock. It seemed like five hours. Someone was forcefully knocking on her front door. Lizabeth crept to the stairs and saw the flashing red light of the cruiser pulsing behind her living room curtains.

Jason shuffled from his room, rubbing his eyes. "There's a police car in front of our house."

Elsie flung her bedroom door open. "Did he come back? Did I miss him again?"

Everyone trooped downstairs and stood behind Lizabeth as she opened the door.

It was Officer Dooley. "We caught your flasher," he said. "We were just going off duty when the call came in. My partner has him cuffed in the cruiser."

"I want to see him," Elsie said. "I want to see what a real pervert looks like."

"Me too," Jason said, following after Elsie. "What's a pervert?"

Lizabeth grabbed a raincoat from the hall closet and ran after Jason. "Jason Kane! You come back here," she yelled, struggling into the raincoat. "You stay away from the pervert! Don't you dare go near that police car!"

Elsie pressed her nose against the cruiser window. "That isn't a pervert," she said disgustedly. "That's Matt."

Lizabeth looked through the window at Matt. "What are you doing in there?"

"I've been arrested."

"Omigod."

"We caught him red-handed," Dooley said. "He was throwing stones at your window."

"I was supposed to come over first thing in the morning to work on her bathroom," Matt said. "She wouldn't answer her door, so I went around back and tried to wake her up by throwing stones at her window."

Lizabeth groaned. "I thought you were a flasher."

Matt grinned at her. "Wishful thinking."

"No. Last night some man showed up in my backyard, and he was only wearing his tie and his shoes. Guess I panicked this morning. I thought he'd come back."

"So what do you think?" Dooley said. "Is this the guy or what?"

Lizabeth shook her head. "The flasher was shorter. Not nearly so muscular. He had sort of a potbelly."

Matt climbed out of the black-and-white cruiser. "He was only wearing his tie and his shoes?"

"A yuppie flasher," Elsie said. "They're the worst kind."

It was getting out of hand, Lizabeth decided. She was beginning to regret calling the police. Now that it was daylight the whole thing seemed silly. The man just stood there with a bag over his head. It was probably a prank, a fraternity initiation, a practical joke. "I'm sure I'll never see him again," Lizabeth said to the gathering. "And if he comes back, I'll send Aunt Elsie out after him."

Dooley looked Elsie over and grinned. "Go easy on him," he said. "Call us if you need help."

Elsie grunted and turned toward the house. "What's in the bag sitting on the porch? Looks like a bakery bag."

Ferguson raced across the lawn, snatched the bag without ever breaking stride, and disappeared down the street.

"Yup," Matt said wistfully. "It was a bakery bag."

Elsie narrowed her eyes. "I could have used a doughnut this morning. Were there any Boston creams?"

"Yup. Fresh from the oven."

"I don't mind that dog sinking his teeth into an old football," Elsie said, "but when he starts swiping my doughnuts, he's gone too far."

"He's just a puppy," Lizabeth said. "He had a traumatic infanthood. He was abandoned on the side of the road."

Matt thought the people who abandoned Ferguson knew what they were doing. He looked like a cross between a schnauzer and a Great Dane, and he had the personality of Attila the Hun. The dog obviously had an eating disorder, and what was he doing when the potbellied degenerate was parading around in his birthday suit? The damn dog probably hadn't given out a single woof. "So he's a puppy, huh? He's pretty big for a puppy."

"Of course he's big," Elsie said. "Worthless dog eats everything in the house. He'd eat a table leg if you put gravy on it."

Lizabeth sat on the closed seat of the toilet and watched Matt run his thumb over a bead of caulking compound at the base of the tub. She leaned forward, resting her elbows on her knees, cupping her chin in her hands. She was close enough to feel the warmth from his body, close enough to see that he had freckles under the fine blond hair on his forearm. It was nice like this, she thought. Even nicer than working together at the construction site. The employer-employee relationship had been replaced by something that was much more relaxed, more intimate, almost conjugal. He was an interesting man, she decided. Sometimes he fit her stereotype of a macho carpenter and sometimes he surprised her with his intelligence and sensitivity. "So what do you like to do when you're not building or repairing houses?"

He stood, wiped his hands on his cutoff jeans, and thought about it. "I watch television. I go to hockey games in Philly. I ride my bike around."

"I saw a hockey game once," Lizabeth said. "I thought the men looked cute in those short pants, but it was horribly violent. They kept beating on each other. I don't understand what men find so fascinating about fighting."

Matt felt his mind go blank. It was a good thing he didn't tell her about his short-lived career in amateur boxing. Or his front-row season passes for the Flyers. Or the time he met Hulk Hogan and almost passed out from excitement. "How about you?" Matt finally said. "What do you do?"

"I used to bake cookies. Does that sound dumb?"

"No. It sounds nice. Very domestic." He thought she looked displeased at that, so he amended his answer. "Very creative."

"Mmmm. Well, I'm not sure what I do now. I still bake cookies, but it's not nearly as satisfying. I suppose I'm at a crossroads."

He sat on the edge of the tub and studied her. "What about childhood dreams? Did you want to be a doctor? Or an astronomer? Did you want to grow up to be a fire chief?"

Lizabeth examined the tube of caulking compound and squeezed out a glob that artlessly landed on her foot. "I was never that realistic about my future. I wanted to be a fairy."

"And did you succeed?"

She laughed. "Not entirely. I'm still working on it. I'm having a hard time with the wings."

"So what are your adult dreams? What do you aspire to now?"

She shrugged. "I don't know. I don't seem to have any aspirations. I suppose I have little goals.

Paying my bills on time. Making a home for my-self and my children. Learning how to caulk a bathtub."

Disappointment prickled in his chest. All her aspirations were of independence. And she hadn't mentioned Paris. If she'd asked the same question of him, he might have said he'd like to get married and have a family. Of course, she'd already done that, so he understood she would want something different. But understanding didn't make it any easier. He decided to change the subject. "So, how do you like construction work?"

"I like it. It's useful. I like being outdoors. The men have been nice to me." She looked into his eyes. "And I like working next to you. You're restoring my interest in the opposite sex." She saw the way his eyebrows raised and his mouth curved into a mercurial smile. "I don't just mean in the sexual sense. My marriage had a lot of painful moments. As the years progressed I reached the sorry conclusion that not only weren't men necessary to happiness, but they were a definite pain in the neck." She shook her head. "I was basing that judgment on very limited experience. There haven't been many men in my life."

"Does this mean I'm not a pain in the neck?"

"No. The part about the pain in the neck still holds. The part about happiness has changed. When we work as a team I feel like all the puzzle pieces fall into place and make a whole. It's comfortable. It makes me happy inside. I decided it has something to do with man-woman chemistry and friendship. We would probably make wonderful love together."

Matt fanned himself with a hand towel. Maybe she would mention the trip to Paris after all.

"Am I making you uncomfortable?"

"Yeah. It feels great."

Jason knocked on the closed bathroom door. "I gotta go."

"Go upstairs," Lizabeth yelled. "Matt's working in here."

Matt looked amused at that.

"I thought you might want to continue the discussion," Lizabeth said.

"About making love?"

"Mmmm. Bathrooms are so intimate. They inspire frankness, don't you think?"

Matt grinned at her. "Have you been drinking?"

"Nope. I've been thinking."

"That's even more dangerous." He stood and pulled her to him. "What else have you been thinking?"

"Uh-uh, it's your turn to think."

His hands spanned her waist, framing her hipbones. "I think I should kiss you."

She felt her stomach tumble. "A man of action, huh?" Their eyes locked for a fraction of a second— long enough for Lizabeth to see the raw hunger, long enough for her to see some other emotion. Annoyance? Their mouths met and all things cerebral were forgotten. Only passion remained. They had both been abstinent far too long. Physically and emotionally abstinent.

His hands roamed her back, pressing her into him, but the closer he held her the more dissatisfied he felt. It was always like this, he thought. He was never able to get enough of her. Never enough talking, never enough laughing, never enough loving. It was the loving he needed now. He needed more. He needed to feel flesh against flesh, not for a stolen moment in a bathroom, but for hours and hours in total privacy.

Someone rapped on the bathroom door and Matt whispered an oath into Lizabeth's hair.

"Yes?"

"I have to use the facilities," Elsie said. "You gonna be done soon?"

Lizabeth took a moment to find her voice. "We'll be done in a minute, Aunt Elsie. Matt's just finishing up in here."

"I bet he is," Elsie said. "When that door opens I better see some fancy caulking."

Matt moved away and gathered his tools. "I think I'm in trouble."

"It's all my fault," Lizabeth said.

Matt handed her an empty container of grout. "Damn right it's all your fault. Next time you want to have a discussion about making love it's going to take place in my house." He saw the panic register in her face. "That suggestion make you nervous?"

"Very."

"You know what you are? You're a tease. Every time you get passionate with me it's in a public place." He tangled his hand in her hair, his thumb stroked across her lower lip, and his voice gentled. "You need to take some time out and come to terms with your own sexuality. And you have to give some serious thought to me. I'm in love with you."

Lizabeth swallowed. "Wow."

Matt opened the bathroom door and nudged her forward. That wasn't so bad, he decided. Now it was out in the open. He said it out loud and his voice hadn't cracked, and he hadn't fainted, and the world hadn't come to an end. He'd broken out into a cold sweat, but he didn't think anyone would notice.

He passed Elsie in the foyer. "You're sweating like a pig," she said. "It must have been hot in there."

Four

Matt was in love with her. She'd run it over in her mind a hundred times in the last three hours, and she still wasn't sure how she felt. It was flattering, of course. And exciting. It was also frightening. And it made her stomach upset. Nerves, she told herself. She wasn't ready. It was all happening too fast. Well, if it was happening too fast it was her own fault. She'd encouraged him. Worse than that, she'd taken the initiative. And he was right about the teasing part. She always managed to lead him on in public places. It hadn't been intentional. Matt called it teasing, and she supposed it might look like that from his point of view, but she knew that sort of teasing wasn't part of her makeup. It was more that she was testing the water, and she'd unconsciously provided herself with a chastity belt. It had been cowardly, she decided.

She closed her eyes and tried to sleep, but sleep wouldn't come. Her curtains were open, allowing the cool evening air to fill her room. Moonlight spilled over her bedroom floor, and Bob the Cat stretched across the bottom of the summer patchwork quilt. "You see what that man has done to my life?" Lizabeth questioned Bob. "He's made me into an insomniac. He's disrupted my emotional stability." It was a nice disruption, she admitted. Her life was immeasurably richer since Matt had come into it. Okay, so if it was so much richer why was she so worried? What was the problem? The problem kept slipping away from her. That didn't mean it didn't exist, she told herself. All it meant was that she wasn't able to nail it down. It sat in the pit of her stomach—a small dark lump of panic that was only noticeable at two in the morning.

The silence was pierced by a woman's scream. It was a scream of outrage, not terror, Lizabeth decided, scrambling to her feet. She heard the sound of someone running, and she reached the window just in time to see the flasher sprint into her yard. He stopped short and looked up at Lizabeth, not bothering with his flashlight. The sky was clear and there was enough moonlight to illuminate the man's pale skin. He stood absolutely still for a split second and then he waved. It was a little wave, the kind you do with just the tips of your fingers and your hand held at shoulder level. Dogs barked throughout the neighborhood, a police siren sounded in the distance, and the man took off at a dead run and disappeared into the night.

Elsie rushed into Lizabeth's room. "Did I hear someone scream? Was that pervert back here?"

"He must have frightened some lady down the street. And then he ran through the yards trying to get away. He stopped only long enough to wave."

"You mean I missed him again?"

"Yup."

Elsie pressed her lips together. "Was he naked?"

"Yup."

"Was he dangerous-looking?"

Lizabeth smiled. "No. He wasn't especially dangerous-looking. In fact, he looked quite harmless." And there was something familiar about him, she thought. Something she couldn't put her finger on.

"It's them harmless-looking ones you have to worry about," Elsie said. "This guy could be a killer. He could be a rapist."

Lizabeth pulled the curtains closed. "I don't think he's a killer. He wouldn't have anyplace to hide the murder weapon."

Matt took a firm grip on his coffee mug. "He came back?"

"No big deal," Lizabeth said. "He ran through the yard and waved to me."

"What about the police? What were the police doing?"

Lizabeth leaned her elbows on the kitchen table and sipped her coffee. "The police were chasing him. They waved to me, too."

"This is a great neighborhood you live in," Matt

said. "Very friendly. Everyone waves to everyone else."

"No need to get sarcastic."

"I'm not sarcastic. I'm worried. I don't like the idea of some nut-case picking you to be his victim."

"He didn't pick me to be his victim last night. He just happened to run through the yard."

Matt scowled into his coffee mug. She should be more frightened. People were careful when they were frightened. They didn't take chances. Lizabeth was talking about this guy in the same tone of voice she used for stories about Ferguson. Next thing she'd be leaving cookies on the picnic table in case Mr. Peekaboo got hungry while he was exposing himself. "So who was the victim last night? Anyone we know?"

"Mmmmm. Angie Kuchta. She lives two houses down."

"Have you spoken to her?"

Lizabeth studied the contents of the doughnut bag and extracted a Boston cream. "Yes. His MO was pretty much the same. He got her attention by throwing stones at her bedroom window. Then he turned the flashlight on her, and when he turned the flashlight on himself she screamed and woke up the entire neighborhood."

"And the police didn't catch him?"

"Nope." Lizabeth bit into her doughnut, and a glob of pudding squeezed out the back end and dropped onto the table.

Ferguson loped in from the living room and cleaned the pudding off the table with one swipe of his huge tongue.

Lizabeth's upper lip curled back. "Oh, gross!"

"Don't worry," Matt said. "I came prepared this time." He handed Ferguson a second bakery bag and opened the back door for the dog. "I hope he likes sticky buns."

Lizabeth poured Lysol on the kitchen table and scrubbed. When she was satisfied the table was clean she sat down and refilled her coffee mug. "There's something odd about all of this." She looked around to make sure they were alone, and she lowered her voice. "Angie's husband was off on a business trip last night. There aren't many single women in this neighborhood, but the flasher hit a woman alone both times. And another thing: How does he always know the right bedroom?"

Matt raised his eyebrows. "You think he could be one of your neighbors?"

Lizabeth thoughtfully chewed her doughnut. "There was something familiar about him. The way he stood, or the way he waved. I don't know."

"Have you told this to the police?"

"I mentioned it to Officer Dooley, but he said he could hardly go door-to-door gathering up men. Also, we have a problem, because the only part Angie and I would definitely recognize is usually covered up in a lineup."

Matt raised his eyebrows. "That *is* a problem."

"Mmmm. And to tell you the truth, I haven't seen very many men, but so far they've all looked pretty much alike down there. I might not even be able to recognize the flasher if he were naked in a crowd."

Matt squinted over the doughnut bag. "Lizabeth, exactly how many men have you seen?"

"Two."

"Does that include the flasher?"

"Yup."

He couldn't stop the smile from creeping across his face. "Would you like to see a third?" He was being flip, but he was secretly pleased. He thought it was nice that she was so selective.

"Would you like a knuckle sandwich?"

He tipped back in his chair and crossed his arms over his chest. "Maybe you wouldn't need to see that part of the flasher. Maybe you could recognize him from his build or his walk or his wave."

"I don't know. I don't feel very confident about that."

"Suppose we gave a barbecue and invited everyone in the neighborhood. You'd get a chance to scope out all the men."

Lizabeth gestured with her half-eaten doughnut. "You know, a barbecue might not be a bad idea. It would give me the opportunity to meet the rest of my neighbors, and who knows, maybe something would click." She turned her attention back to the doughnut, giving it a look of sublime appreciation. "Yum," she said, flicking her tongue at the chocolate icing.

Matt felt his blood pressure suddenly skyrocket. He'd known his share of women. He'd seen them wallowing in Jell-O, floundering in mud, and dancing on bars . . . and he'd never had a problem with the fit of his slacks in public. But watching Lizabeth strip a doughnut of its icing had him squirming in his seat.

She finished the doughnut and looked at him expectantly. "Something wrong? You look all flushed."

"I'm fine," Matt said. "Why don't we go over to my house and make plans."

"For the barbecue?"

"Yeah, that too."

"We can make plans right here," Lizabeth said. "I'll go get some paper and a pencil."

He put his hand over hers to stop her from getting up. "I need privacy to make these plans. I need time. Lots of time."

"Matthew Hallahan, you're not talking about a barbecue, are you?"

"Listen, Lizabeth, I'm in a bad way. How close are you to finding yourself? Maybe if we both looked, we could find you faster."

"I don't think finding myself is a group activity."

"Why not?"

"Because you don't assert your independence by asking someone to help you. This is something I have to do by myself. I need time . . ."

"How much time?"

Lizabeth rolled her eyes. "I don't know how much time! This isn't something I can set a deadline on. Maybe a week, maybe a month, maybe a year."

"A year! I can't wait a year. I'll be dead in a year. I have an incurable disease. You have to help me."

Lizabeth grinned at him. "What's the name of this disease?"

"Infatuation. The symptoms would be a lot less painful if we were alone together in my bedroom." He brought her hand to his mouth and kissed a fingertip.

Lizabeth felt the heat shoot through her. She watched him move onto another fingertip and surprised herself by moaning out loud when he took the finger in his mouth and circled it with his tongue. She immediately snatched her hand away.

"You sure you wouldn't like to fool around a little?"

"Of course I'd like to fool around a little. I like you. And I'm attracted to you." Saying that she liked Matt Hallahan and was attracted to him was such an understatement it bordered on a lie, Lizabeth decided. Why she felt compelled to hold him at a distance was beyond her, except that she really hadn't known him very long. And what she did know about him showed they were very different. A serious relationship was tough enough without the additional burden of different life-styles and educational backgrounds. It was the first time she'd articulated the thought, even to herself, and it hit her like an Acme safe falling on Road Runner. She wondered if that was the problem eating away at her stomach every night. Different life-styles and educational backgrounds. She'd graduated from Amherst and Matt had a tattoo on his forearm. Lizabeth Kane, she silently whispered, you're a snob. You've met the man of your dreams, and you're holding him at arm's length because he's a carpenter. Could that be true? She'd never thought of herself as a snob before, and she didn't like the way it fit. It was something she'd have to chew on when she was alone.

Matt watched her with raised eyebrows. "Well?"

"I have to give this some consideration."

"Listen, if it's a morality thing about prenuptial sex I could fix it. We could get married. I know a justice of the peace who works on Sunday . . ."

"No!" Lizabeth cleared her throat and lowered her voice. "I'm not ready to get married. I had one bad marriage, and I don't want another. I don't want to rush into something I might regret later. Besides, I have a suspicion that if I said 'yes' to your proposal you'd take the first train out of town. You're playing with me."

There was some truth to that, Matt thought. He could afford to be bold about commitment, knowing she'd reject him, but he didn't think he'd take the first train out of town. Impossible as it seemed, even to him, he actually wanted to get married. "Okay, so let's go over this then. You like me. You might even decide you love me after due deliberation." He was ticking each point off on his fingers. "You don't want to rush into another marriage. And you obviously don't want to rush into what might be an incredibly passionate but purely physical relationship."

Lizabeth gave a sigh of relief. He understood. "Yes."

"How far do you want to go?"

"Pardon?"

"I thought it would be helpful to set some boundaries. Just to make everything clear. So I know exactly how far I can go."

Relief turned to alarm. "Do we have to decide that now?"

"I don't want to make any mistakes. I assume kissing is all right."

"Kissing is fine."

He leaned across the table. "With tongues?"

She felt the flush beginning to creep up from her shirt collar. "Tongues are okay."

"How about touching? What body parts am I allowed to touch?" His eyes dropped to her chest. "Can I touch your breasts?"

Lizabeth unconsciously pressed her knees together. "I don't think this is necessary right now . . ."

"Can I take your shirt off? Can I—"

Lizabeth smacked him on the side of the head with the doughnut bag. "Listen up. I am not going to bed with you. As far as I'm concerned, anything up to that point is fair game, but I put the burden of stopping on you. You are totally responsible for maintaining my virtue."

"That's rotten!" Matt narrowed his eyes and grinned malevolently. "You're doing this because you have no willpower. You're putting the burden on me because you're afraid once you get going you won't be able to stop."

"Yup. That's true."

"Heh, heh, heh."

Lizabeth picked up her coffee cup and took a sip, looking at him over the rim. "You don't scare me. You're an honorable person and you're supposedly in love with me."

"Yes, but I'm also a desperate man."

"So you're telling me you'd take advantage of me when I was in a weakened position?"

"Damn right!"

Elsie came in for another doughnut. "What's going on in here?"

"We're making plans for a barbecue," Lizabeth said. "We're going to invite the whole neighborhood."

"I'm not going to have to cook for this, am I? Don't think I'm making potato salad for two hundred people."

Lizabeth shook her head. "We'll ask everyone to bring something—a dessert or a covered dish. And we'll provide the hot dogs. We can borrow a couple of grills."

Elsie pulled a cherry Danish out of the bag. "Sounds like a pain in the behind to me. You got some good reason for having this shindig?"

Lizabeth hesitated, debating whether to confide in Elsie. Elsie wasn't known for her ability to keep secrets. Not that it really mattered this time. In fact, maybe it was for the best if the flasher knew he was about to be found out. "I thought if I got all the men in the neighborhood together I might recognize the flasher."

Elsie's eyes sparkled in approval. "You're from the Hawkins side all right. We don't just sit around on our butt. No sir, we go out and get the job done. You think we need to have a gun on hand in case he gets unruly? I'm real good with a gun."

"No guns!" Lizabeth stood at her seat, palms flat on the table, and leaned toward Elsie to make her point. "I don't want any guns in this house."

Elsie bit into her doughnut. "I suppose it wouldn't be neighborly to shoot him, anyway."

"And the police would frown on it," Lizabeth said. "They're not fond of vigilantes."

Elsie turned her attention to Matt. "Did you come over here just to plan a barbecue?"

"No. It's supposed to rain tonight, so I thought I'd take a look at the roof. I might be able to patch some of the worst spots."

Lizabeth caught her bottom lip between her teeth. "You don't have to go up on the roof to do that, do you?"

"Worried about me?" Matt asked, looking pleased.

"Of course I'm worried. The roof is a mess. The tiles are loose and the wood is probably rotted. If you fall off and get hurt they'll raise the rates on my homeowner's insurance."

He drained his coffee cup and rose. "I'll keep all that in mind."

"Do you need help?"

"You bet. I need someone to hold the ladder." He slung his arm around Lizabeth's shoulders and dragged her out of the kitchen. "Holding the ladder is a very important job. Not just anyone can do it. It has to be someone you trust."

"Uh-huh."

"And if you turn out to be good at holding the ladder, later on I might let you hold something else."

Lizabeth's stomach did a rollover. "I'm not sure I want to hear this."

He turned and pinned her against the front door. "Lizzy Kane, you have a dirty mind."

He was silently laughing, and his mouth was just inches away. She could feel his chest crush into hers, feel the soft denim of his jeans slide between her bare legs, feel his heart thumping behind his black T-shirt. "You set me up," Lizabeth said.

His face was a study in offended innocence. "Not true. I was thinking you could hold my shirt if it gets too warm on the roof, or you could hold my hammer while I carry the shingles." He leaned even closer, and his mouth settled onto hers in lazy possession. He slid his tongue along the inside of her upper lip and pulled away just enough to be able to look into her eyes. "You were the one who thought about holding more intimate objects," he whispered. "You want to know what I think? I think you want to hold my—"

Lizabeth made a strangled sound in the back of her throat.

"Something wrong?" Matt asked. "I thought talking was okay. I thought everything was allowed except the ultimate act."

She felt her temper flare. He was seeing how far he could push. Well, that was great. Two could play that game. "Fine," Lizabeth said. "You want to play hardball?"

He was close enough for her to feel the laughter rumbling deep in his chest.

"No," he said. "There's no doubt in my mind that I'd lose."

"Really? Scared of me, huh?"

"Yup. I'm in love with you, and that makes me vulnerable. If you wanted, you could squash me like a bug. You could trample my ego flat."

"I bet when you were a kid you got away with murder," Lizabeth said.

Matt propped the ladder securely against the house. "What makes you think that?"

"You know all the right things to say to disarm a woman. You probably had your mother wrapped around your little finger."

"Hardly. I was the fifth kid in a family of seven. Half the time my mother couldn't remember my name."

To Lizabeth it seemed like a bitter statement to make, but there was no bitterness in his voice. In fact, there was no inflection at all. The tone had been flat. Matter-of-fact. His eyes, usually so filled with feeling, were blank, and his face held the sort of vacuous expression that came with denial or followed unbearable pain. There's been a tragedy here, Lizabeth thought. And it has been dealt with and filed away. She didn't want to drag it out and open old wounds.

She silently searched for something to say, but found nothing. She wanted to hug him, but she wasn't sure if he'd like that. It was so much easier with children, she thought. You could ease their hurt with a kiss and by holding them close. You could tuck a little boy under your arm and read him a book and chase all the dragons away, but men were much more complicated. From her limited experience she realized men had a strange ego that one had to contend with. And they had weird ideas about what represented weakness. Her ex-husband had detested her protective instincts. Not that she wanted to judge all men by Paul, but it was all she had to go on.

Matt watched her slim hands nervously twisting the hem of her T-shirt. Great, he thought, good going, Hallahan. He had made her feel bad. "Look, don't worry about it. It's no big deal. My childhood left something to be desired, but it's behind me."

"I didn't mean to pry."

He took her in his arms and held her close, pressing a kiss into the curls at the top of her head. "It's okay if you pry. You're allowed. When you grow up in a family of seven kids you get used to people prying. Privacy was an unknown quantity in my life."

"Wouldn't that make you want to guard it all the more?"

Matt's mouth twisted into a wry grin. "No. Mostly what I guarded was my underwear. I had four brothers who all wore the same size."

"I guess that pretty much puts things in perspective," Lizabeth said. "It always helps to have your priorities straight."

"You have any brothers or sisters?"

She shook her head. "No. I was the pampered, overprotected only child."

Matt squatted while he opened a box of shingles. "These aren't going to match exactly, but at least they'll keep the rain out." He looked up at her, his lopsided grin giving his features a rakish quality. "Did you wear pretty dresses and bows in your hair and white socks with lace on the cuff?"

Lizabeth laughed. "Yes, but the effect was usually marred by skinned knees, unruly hair, and grass stains on my skirt. I was a completely unmanageable child. One time I tied a tablecloth around my shoulders and jumped out of a tree Superman style and broke my leg."

"But mostly you wanted to be a fairy."

She was surprised he had remembered. "Yes.

Fairies were my favorites. A fairy isn't afraid of anything," Lizabeth said. "A fairy just grabs life by the throat."

"That's not what I heard. I heard fairies were outrageously promiscuous. I heard they grabbed life about two and a half feet lower."

"Hmmmm. Well, I suppose there are all kinds of fairies, just as there are all kinds of carpenters. Some are undoubtedly more sexually oriented than others."

Five

Lizabeth snatched her clock in the darkened room and held the luminous dial close to her face. One-thirty. And Elsie was still sitting in the rocking chair by the window. "Aunt Elsie," Lizabeth said. "If you're that desperate to see a naked man I'll rent you one. I swear, if you'll just go to bed I'll thumb through the yellow pages first thing in the morning. I might even be able to find one that dances or does aerobics."

Elsie rocked with her feet flat and her knees spread. She got a good push off that way. "You know what's wrong with these damn perverts?" she said. "You can't count on them. No consideration for other people." She rocked forward in front of the sheer white curtains and back into the black shadows. She rocked steady as a metronome. "Grrrch," the chair went back. "Slap," her feet hit the floor coming forward. "Grrrch," "slap," "grrrch," "slap," "grrrch," "slap."

Lizabeth buried her face in the pillow and groaned. She had to go to work tomorrow. She needed sleep. She needed peace and quiet. She wasn't used to old ladies rocking the night away in a corner of her room. "He's flashed for two nights now," Lizabeth said. "Maybe he's tired. Maybe he's taking a night off."

"Damn pervert," Elsie said. "He should be locked up. He should be ashamed of himself for going around terrorizing defenseless women."

"You don't seem very terrorized," Lizabeth observed.

"Yeah, but I'm a Hawkins. You know us Hawkinses are tougher than most. It takes more than a naked man to terrorize a Hawkins."

A stone pinged at the window and Elsie stopped rocking. There was silence in the room while both women held their breath, waiting for another stone to hit. Lizabeth crept from her bed and pulled the curtain aside. A spot of light slid across the window, briefly illuminating Lizabeth. There was darkness for a moment, and then the flasher turned the light on himself.

Elsie let out a small gasp. "Well, will you look at that!" she whispered. "The man's standing there just as bold as could be in his birthday suit!" Her eyes narrowed. "The nerve of that man! Don't this beat all." She moved a fraction of an inch closer to the window. "Is that all he does? He just stands there?"

"Yup."

"Don't it get boring?"

"Yup."

Elsie watched him for a moment longer. "I suppose it's a good thing he's not dangerous. If he were dangerous I'd feel like I had to get my forty-five and blast him one."

"Don't even think about it. Nobody's getting blasted from my window."

"Nothing to worry about. I don't shoot to kill. I always aim for the privates. Nothing a pervert hates more than to get shot in the privates."

"Yeah," Lizabeth said, trying not to smile. "That'd put a crimp in his style."

Elsie mournfully shook her head. "I'm a pretty good shot, but I'd have a hard time with this guy—he hasn't got much of a target. No wonder the poor man wears a bag over his head." She looked hopefully at her niece. "Don't it ever get more exciting?"

"Not so far."

"Well," Elsie said, "thank heaven for small favors." She grasped the screen and slid it up into the top half of the window so she could lean out. "Hey, you damn pervert," she yelled at the man. "You should be ashamed of yourself, going around showing everybody your business. Haven't you got anything better to do than to stand there looking like a damn fool?"

There was an audible gasp of breath from the flasher, the light blinked out, and the man ran off, crashing through the juniper and azalea bushes that bordered the backyard.

"Ow," Elsie said, "that's gotta smart."

"I should never have told you," Lizabeth shouted after Matt. "You're making a mountain out of a molehill."

Matt looped a length of electrical cable over his shoulder. "That's what Elsie said. But I don't care what body proportions this flasher has, I don't want him coming near you." He handed a two-hundred-watt floodlight to his electrician and pointed to the large oak at the rear of Lizabeth's property. "I want a flood installed there and the cable run underground. I want one at either end of the house . . ."

"This is *my* house," Lizabeth said, running to keep up with Matt. "You can't just come into my yard and take over. You can't tell me what to do with my house."

"When's your birthday?"

"November third."

He grabbed her by the shoulders and dragged her to him. He kissed her long and hard and released her. "Happy birthday," he said. "It wouldn't be polite to refuse a birthday present, would it?"

"I don't like being bullied."

"You're not being bullied," Matt said. "You're being protected. And if this doesn't scare him off, I'm moving in."

Lizabeth stuffed her fists onto her hips and glared at him. "I'm perfectly capable of taking care of myself."

Matt handed the cable to the electrician. "I want a switch installed in her bedroom and in the kitchen." He looked down at Lizabeth and grinned. "Damned if you aren't cute when you get all riled up like this."

"And another thing: You kept calling me 'honey' at work today. What will the men think?"

"I wouldn't worry about it. None of those men think while they're working."

"And it was very nice of you to have that fancy restaurant cater lunch for me, but I felt a little conspicuous."

"I swear, I didn't order the violin player," Matt said, raising his hand. "They threw him in as a bonus."

Lizabeth shot him an intensely peeved look.

"All right, all right. I admit, I've gone off the deep end. I have this horrible compulsion to do things for you. I can't control myself. Boy, I tell you, love is hell."

"Oh yeah? If it's such hell why don't you sound more miserable? You've been looking absolutely smug all day. And predatory. I have a cat. I've watched *Wild Kingdom*. I know predatory when I see it."

"I have a plan," Matt said.

He was wearing a navy T-shirt with the sleeves cut out, and it tucked into jeans that were almost white from wear. The jeans had a frayed, horizontal slash across the knee and were perfectly molded to masculine bulges and hard, muscular thighs. He smelled like pine sawdust and musk, and Lizabeth thought he was the sexiest thing she'd ever seen. If his plan was half as enticing as his perfect butt, she was in big trouble. "What's the plan?"

"You might not want to hear it. It involves sweaty, naked bodies . . . ours. And there's this part where you're on fire—internally, of course—and you're begging me to make hard, passionate love to you."

"That's not a plan. That's a fantasy."

Matt smiled. "Not the way I see it."

Elsie pulled into the driveway in her big blue-

and-white Cadillac. She levered herself out of the car, took a grocery bag from the front seat, and started across the lawn. "What's going on here?" she said. "What's all the fuss about?"

Lizabeth took the bag from her. "Matt's having lights installed around the house for security purposes."

Elsie smiled broadly, creasing her face. "Good idea. It was a shame we had to miss that guy bashing his way through the azalea bushes last night."

"It's a waste of time and money," Lizabeth said. "He'll probably never come back. And besides, it's supposed to rain tonight. No one would be dumb enough to flash in the rain."

Eight hours later, Lizabeth admitted she'd been wrong about the flasher. There seemed to be no limit to his stupidity. Rain softly pattered on the windowpane and ran in narrow rivulets down the screen while Lizabeth and Elsie peered out at the bedraggled exhibitionist. His paper-bag mask sat limp and wet on his head, his tie was plastered to his chest, and his docksiders were sunk a good inch and a half in mud.

Elsie slowly shook her head. "That's pathetic."

"He seems a little compulsive about this flashing stuff," Lizabeth said. "I really didn't think he'd show."

"Yeah, you gotta give him something for hanging in there. The man's no quitter."

Lizabeth gnawed on her lower lip. "You think we should throw an umbrella out to him?"

"No," Elsie said, "I kinda like watching him drip. Let's see what he looks like with the floods on him." She reached over and flipped the switch, and the yard was bathed in an eerie wash of white light.

For the first time, the man's arms and legs and shoulders were clearly revealed. Lizabeth thought he seemed much more naked and sadly vulnerable. He took a step backward, then turned and ran around the far side of the house. "This was mean," Lizabeth said. "I think we scared him."

Elsie closed the curtains and stepped back from the window. "You know, as far as perverts go, he isn't much."

Lizabeth smeared joint compound over the last nail in the drywall and stuffed the wooden handle of her six-inch taping knife into her back pocket. Rain thrummed on the roof of the half-finished house and beat against the newly installed Thermopanes, and the cloying smell of wet wood and joint compound mingled with the pungent aroma of freshly turned earth. It was three o'clock, and the light filtering into the upstairs bedroom was weak. It would have been a dismal day, Lizabeth thought, if she hadn't been working side by side with Matt. He had a way of filling a room so that even the most barren space seemed snug and inviting.

"So what do you think about drywall?" Matt asked. "Is this intellectually stimulating, or what?"

Lizabeth smiled. Four hours of slathering white goop over nails was not intellectually stimulating, but it was just fine for her purposes. It gave her a lot of time to think about other things. Not the least of which was the flasher. Ridiculous as it seemed, she felt sorry for him. Undoubtedly, flashing was some form of aggression, just as rape was, and she had to always keep that in mind, she told herself. And this wasn't a random flashing. That made it all the more frightening. So why wasn't she afraid? Why did she feel like a crumb for turning the lights on him? And then there was Matt. Thinking about Matt had become a full-time job. She thought about him at night when she was alone in bed, and she thought about him first thing in the morning when she brushed her teeth. Lizabeth burst out laughing, because in a moment of insight she realized she was much more frightened of Matt than she was of the flasher.

Matt raised his eyebrows. "Yes?"

"I was thinking of the flasher," Lizabeth said. "And it occurred to me that I'm much more frightened of you than I am of him."

Matt stomped the lid down on the can of joint compound. "There's all kinds of fear," he said. "Some kinds of fear are much more fun than others."

It was true, Lizabeth thought. Matt was a ride down a white-water canyon. He could make her stomach drop with a sideways glance or a small, knowing smile. Danger had its up side, she decided. There was nothing like an occasional shot of adrenaline to spice up your life. Lizabeth, Lizabeth, Lizabeth, a small voice whispered, those are fairy thoughts. Better watch out, the voice continued; before you know it you'll be eating Swiss chocolates for breakfast and wearing silk underpants. Hah! Lizabeth answered. Fat chance, on her salary.

Matt reached out for her, but she slipped away. "So, why are you afraid of me?"

"First of all, there's sex. It makes me nervous."

"Everyone's a little nervous in the beginning." He grinned.

"No," Lizabeth said, "you don't understand. I mean *really* nervous. The truth is, I'm not especially good at it past a certain point." She rolled her eyes and groaned.

The grin widened. "Bet I could fix that."

Lizabeth didn't doubt it for a second. "Maybe we should continue this conversation some other time."

Matt looped an arm around her. "How about I take you home and check on the roof to make sure there are no leaks. Then I can say hello to the kids and investigate the contents of the oven to see if I want to stay for supper."

"You think you can get an invitation?"

"Elsie likes me. She growls a lot, but she's a sweet old broad."

Lizabeth giggled. "I'm going to tell her you said that."

"You wouldn't dare! I'll give you five dollars not to tell her."

They both stopped at the door and looked out at the rain. Boards had been laid, from the small cement front porch, across the quagmire that would one day be a lawn, to the curb where Matt's truck was parked. Matt walked across without thinking, as surefooted as a mountain goat, and Lizabeth tiptoed behind him, using her arms for balance, feeling like a high-wire act, wondering at what point in her life she'd lost her sense of daring and balance. When she got to the end of the board Matt was waiting for her with his hands on his hips. "Lizzy," he said, "you walk like a sissy."

"I know," Lizabeth wailed. "I'm not good at this."

"You lack confidence. You have to grab life by the throat. Be a fairy! Besides, what's the worst thing that could happen? You could fall off into the mud. It's not like it's life-threatening."

Rain was beginning to soak into the back of her shirt. "I'm getting wet!"

"Ignore it. Go back and walk on the board like a fairy."

Lizabeth swiped at the water that was dripping from her nose. "A fairy wouldn't walk. A fairy would fly."

"Fairies can't fly in the rain. It's not good for their wings."

"Get out of my way," Lizabeth said. "You don't know squat about fairies, and I don't want to walk on this dumb board anymore."

Matt flapped his arms and made chicken sounds. Lizabeth squeezed her eyes shut. "Uh! Okay, okay. I'll do it."

"Now skip," Matt yelled when she was halfway back to the house. "Jump up and down. Let's see you run!"

Lizabeth giggled and jumped up and down. She was soaked through, and she felt ridiculous. "There," she said, "but I'm not going to run. The board is too slippery. I'll fall."

"I'll catch you."

He was crazy, she thought. And she loved him. And he was right. All she needed was confidence. "This is kinda fun," she yelled to him. "You look awful. You're all wet."

"I know," he yelled back. "You look great."

Lizabeth jumped onto the board with both feet and ran flat out into his arms. The momentum knocked them back into the truck, where they clung together, laughing. "You were wonderful," Matt said. "You had real style out there."

Lizabeth wriggled against him. "I know. I'm a class act."

Their eyes held and his mouth very deliberately settled on hers. It was warm and wet with the rain, and his hands possessively moved across her water-slicked back. In all her years of marriage to Paul, nothing had ever felt this intimate, this loving. If nothing more comes of this relationship, Lizabeth thought, at least I'll have had this afternoon. She couldn't imagine it getting any better. It was already perfect.

"I hate to put a damper on things," Matt said, "but you're breaking out in goose bumps. I think I should get you into some dry clothes."

Lizabeth swung into the truck cab and shook the rain from her hair. She waited until Matt settled behind the wheel before talking. "I suppose, since you're going home with me, and you're going to find out anyway . . . I suppose I should tell you the flasher stopped by last night."

Matt turned in her direction, one arm over the back of the bench seat. "He stopped by?"

"Yeah, you know, out in the yard, just like always."

"In the rain?" There was a note of disbelief in his voice.

"It was kind of sad. He was all wet. His tie was soaked, and his bag got soggy."

Matt pressed his lips together. "What about the lights?"

"We turned them on, and he ran away."

"Did you recognize him?"

She shook her head. "No. But I have a much better idea what he looks like. I got to see a lot more of him."

"Wonderful." He put the truck in gear, turned the heater on full blast to warm Lizabeth, and pulled out of the cul-de-sac. "The man is a fruit-cake, Lizabeth. Normal people do not go flashing in the rain."

"Yes, but I think he's a harmless fruitcake. Where are we going? My house is in the opposite direction."

"We're going to my town house. We're going to get some of my clothes, and then we're going back to your place. This guy's flashing career is coming to an end."

"Just exactly what are you going to do?"

"I'm going to spend the night with you. I'm going to wait for the flasher to appear. Then I'm going to break every bone in his body."

"No! You can't do that. He's not a violent person. He's just a little misguided. I think you should talk to him."

"Talk to him?" Was she kidding? "Fine, if that's what you want, I'll talk to him. First I'll rip the bag off his head, then I'll grab him by his lousy tie, and then I'll talk to him. I'll tell him if he ever comes within a quarter of a mile of you, I'll break every bone in his body."

Lizabeth crossed her arms over her chest and slunk down in the seat. She made a disgusted sound with her tongue and stonily stared out the truck window.

"Now what?" Matt asked. "I agreed to talk to him. Now what's wrong?"

"Threatening to break every bone in his body isn't talking to him. It's macho garbage."

"Macho garbage?" His face creased into a broad grin.

"Unh!" Lizabeth rolled her eyes. "You know what you are? You're a . . . a carpenter!"

"What's that supposed to mean?"

"Big shoulders, nifty butt, no brains. It means you have to prove your manhood with a display of muscle."

"You think I have a nifty butt?" He sounded pleased.

"Have you been listening?" Lizabeth shouted.

"Yup. The part about the no brains isn't true. I may not have a fancy education, but I'm not stupid. The rest of it I suppose is okay." He parked in a numbered space and pointed to a brick-front town house. "That's mine. Number twenty-two." The rain had slackened off to a fine drizzle. Matt went around the truck and opened the door for Lizabeth. "Come on. This is your big opportunity to see what sort of house a macho garbage man lives in."

"I'm sorry about the macho garbage part. I got carried away. Are you insulted?"

"No. You're probably right. Sometimes I definitely have macho garbage tendencies." He unlocked the front door and followed Lizabeth into the small foyer.

Lizabeth looked into an empty living room. There was no furniture, no rug, no curtains. Just a motorcycle. "There's a motorcycle in your living room."

"I don't have a garage."

"Ah-hah," she said, trying to sound as if his explanation was perfectly ordinary and logical. But her mind was in total chaos. My lord, she thought, he owns a motorcycle. A big, black, shiny motorcycle. She'd never actually known anyone who owned a motorcycle, and she equated this sort of motorcycle with men who drank motor oil and robbed convenience stores. She was in love with a man who had a tattoo and owned a motorcycle! A man who wanted to beat up on an innocent flasher. Of course, he was also the man who set her on fire with his kisses and encouraged her to run and jump in the rain. A man who bought sticky buns for her dog and played soccer with her kids. She chewed on her lower lip and stared at him. "Do you belong to one of those gangs?"

"A bikers' club?" He chuckled. "No. That's not my style." He took her hand and led her upstairs. "Mostly I live up here. I don't do much entertaining, so it might be a little messy." He stopped at the head of the stairs and looked around. "Actually, it's messier than I thought. Maybe you don't want to see this."

The upstairs consisted of two bedrooms and a bath, and laundry was everywhere. It littered the hall, rolled from under furniture like giant dust bunnies, and gathered big time in corners. It spilled out of open closet doors and open drawers and hung from bedposts, doorknobs, and chair backs. One bedroom housed a desk and an upholstered executive swivel chair. The remainder of the room held stacked boxes of floor tile, cans of house paint, heavy-duty extension cords, an as-

sortment of power tools, rolls of duct tape, and
three stacks of old copies of *National Geographic*.
The other room had a dresser, double bed with
night table, and an overstuffed easy chair. A television and VCR had been placed on the dresser,
along with a hot plate and hot-air popcorn maker.
An assortment of crushed beer cans, crumpled
Styrofoam burger boxes, and balled-up bakery bags
mixed with the mounds of clothes on the floor, on
the bed, on the dresser, in the chair.

"It sort of got away from me," Matt said.

Lizabeth shook her head. "Oinkus Americanus.
I've seen this phenomenon before." She unconsciously picked up a T-shirt and folded it. "This is
probably the real reason you want to move into
my house for the night. You've lost your bed." She
folded another T-shirt and stacked it neatly on
the first one.

Matt rooted through a closet and came up with
a maroon gym bag. He kicked at the clothes on
the floor and found a pair of jeans and a yellow
shirt. He put them in the bag with underwear
and socks, and then headed for the bathroom. "It
isn't usually this bad. I've been busy. I've had a lot
on my mind."

"Like what?"

He reappeared with the bag. "You. Me. Other
things."

"What other things?"

"For starters, my partner is still in the hospital.
He'll be in traction another week, and when he
gets out it'll be at least a month before he's back
on the job. He did all the paperwork. He did the
buying and selling. I did the building. Now I'm

stuck with everything. You think this room is a mess, you should take a look at my desk drawers."

"That bad?"

"I should hire a secretary, but Frank will be back in six weeks, and it would take me longer than that to bring someone new up to speed."

Lizabeth finished folding and arranging into neat piles the clothes on the bed. Without thinking, she moved on to the debris on the floor, grouping it into washing categories—darks, whites, hopeless. He was overworked, and some of it was her fault. He'd been spending every minute of his spare time fixing her dilapidated house. She found a wastebasket and began collecting beer cans, deciding some of them had been there since 1985. While she might be partially to blame for the condition of his bedroom, she thought to herself, there were also other forces at work here. Matthew Hallahan was a domestic slob.

"Gee, you're really good at this," Matt said. "I guess you do this folding stuff all the time, huh?"

"When I got married I promised to love, honor, and fold. Folding was the only part that survived." Lizabeth stopped for a moment and looked around. The room was neater now. She was able to see parts of the floor and almost all of the dresser. There was a sense of order to the room, but there was also the feeling that no one lived there. There were no pictures on the walls. No photographs of Matt with a kid brother, no trophies from Little League, no souvenirs from his hitch in the Navy. "Have you lived here very long?" she asked.

"Four or five years." He thought about it for a minute. "No, that's not right. I got out of the Navy and roomed with Frank for two years. Then Frank got married, and I moved in here. I guess I've lived here for . . . ten years." He shook his head in amazement and zipped the gym bag closed. "This was supposed to be temporary. I always intended to build a house for myself, but I just never got around to it. I was always too busy building houses for other people."

"Would you still like to build a house for yourself?"

"I'd like to have a home. A real home. But it's not so important that I build it myself." The people are the important part, Matt thought. He could live in a tent, a tin shack, or the backseat of Elsie's Cadillac, and if Lizabeth was beside him it would be home. He watched her give an involuntary shiver and noticed her lips had turned purple. "Cold?"

"I'm freezing. I've got to get out of these wet clothes."

Matt found a set of clean gray sweats on the bed. "Go take a hot shower. Steam yourself until you're as red as a lobster, and then you can wear my sweats home."

Lizabeth hesitated. "It's only a fifteen-minute drive to my house. I can take a shower there."

"No way. If I bring you home like this Elsie'll yell at me."

He had a point. She clamped her teeth together to keep them from chattering and headed for the bathroom. "I'll only be a minute."

Twenty minutes later Matt listened to the whir of his hair drier, and decided he liked the sound of Lizabeth sharing his bathroom. And he liked the way his bedroom looked without three months' worth of clothes and garbage on the floor. He'd put the dirty laundry into a laundry basket and filed the folded clean clothes away in his bureau. He'd taken Lizabeth's wet clothes to the basement and stuffed them into his clothes drier, and then he'd dragged the vacuum up from the cellar and sucked up clots of dust, crushed corn chips, petrified popcorn, and three spiders that had set up housekeeping. He'd put clean sheets on his bed and was fluffing a red-plaid comforter when Lizabeth sauntered out of the bathroom.

"That was an all-time great shower," she said lazily. "I never have enough hot water at home, and there's always a little person waiting for me on the other side of the door, and you have one of those fancy shower-massage things. It was wonderful."

He wasn't sure if it was the pink tinge to her cheeks, or the silky curls that framed her face, or the way his sweats draped over her delicate bones and clung to her soft curves. It might have been her smile. He was always undone by her smile. And it might have been the intimacy of smelling his soap on her warm skin. The exact reason for Matt's discomfort wasn't clear, but the result was fast becoming obvious. His tongue felt thick and useless, his throat dry, his breathing shallow. His heart galloped in his chest so that he could feel the blood coursing through him in hot waves. In his entire body only one part was working efficiently, and he was thankful it was contained by navy briefs that had shrunk in the drier and by a pair of sturdy jeans.

Lizabeth shuffled across the room in her bare

feet, flopped on the freshly made bed, and closed her eyes. "I can't remember the last time I was this relaxed."

Matt didn't say a word. Didn't move. Couldn't think beyond wanting her. Food, water, shelter—all seemed trivial compared to his need for Lizabeth. He ached with love, and he burned with desire. He shoved his hands into his pockets and wondered if she'd been serious about holding him responsible for her morals.

Lizabeth was suddenly aware of the silence. She propped herself up on one elbow and looked at him. His face was dark with an undefinable emotion. His blond eyebrows were drawn together. A muscle jumped in his jaw. Her gaze slid downward, and she discovered the source of his dilemma. "Oh, Matt!" She pulled a pillow over her face to muffle a giggle.

"This is no laughing matter."

"I can see that!"

"Listen, Lizabeth, we have a very large problem here . . ."

She coyly lowered her lashes. "It's not nice to brag."

Matt slowly shook his head and wagged his finger at her. "You're flirting with me and that's very dangerous because, as you may have noticed, we're alone and my self-control is reaching an all-time low."

"Mmmmm," Lizabeth said, smiling, feeling outrageously bold. She wore no underwear, and the borrowed sweats were softly abrasive against her skin. It was a new sensation. Sexy, she thought. Just right for sprawling on Matt's bed. She real-

ized she wanted to make love with him and acknowledged that she'd come a long way in a very
short time. She wasn't nervous, or embarrassed,
or afraid. For the first time in her life she was
deliciously aroused, and she thought it conve-
nient that his self-control was reaching its all-
time low just when her own sexuality was beginning
to bloom. She watched him crawl across the bed
and straddle her, and she willed herself to relax.
She knew things would be different with Matt. He
knew when to give and when to take, and he
honestly enjoyed both.

He kissed her tenderly, fully intending to be a
slow, sensitive lover. The kiss deepened. Tongue
slid over tongue and hunger took over. In an instant his hands were under her shirt, covering
her breasts, gently squeezing, his thumbs teasing
across rigid nipples. He put his mouth to her
heated skin, trailing kisses from her breasts to
below the waistband of the sweatpants. Too fast,
he thought, but he couldn't stop. He had to see
her. All of her. He had to taste all of her. Clothes
were stripped away and he kissed her again. Lower
this time. Lord, how he wanted her. The wanting
pounded in his groin, and his blood boiled with
it. His kisses grew rough. His mouth was relent-
less as she arched her back and moaned for more.
He felt her shudder and cry out and then he was
inside her, driven by a need almost frightening in
its intensity. Afterward he held her close, afraid
to move from her, afraid he'd been all muscle and
blind passion and no brain.

Her first thought, when she was finally capable
of thought, was that she no longer gave a damn

about being a fairy. She'd just been to the top and anything else, fairy wings included, would be cold potatoes. Her second thought was that she loved Matt Hallahan beyond reason. She loved him when he was gentle and when he was fierce, and she loved him most of all when he was naked. He was magnificent when he was naked.

Matt buried his face in her hair. "Liz, I think I got carried away . . ."

"Mmmmm," Lizabeth said, her voice muffled as she snuggled closer.

"Was it awful?"

"Awful?" She pushed back enough to look at him. "Awful?" She saw he was serious, and his fear prompted a smile.

It was the most radiant smile ever. Filled with love and pride and supreme satisfaction. It was the smile he'd promised himself the first time he saw her. "Hmmm," he said. "So I guess it wasn't awful."

Her smile grew sly and she dallied with a moist curl, wondering how it could be so dark, almost black, when the rest of his hair was so blond. "It was passable," she said.

"You think it could get better if we practiced?"

Lizabeth didn't think she could live through it if it got any better. "Probably it would take a *lot* of practice," she said, letting a fingertip wander lower, provoking a sharp intake of breath.

Almost an hour later, Lizabeth barely had the energy to dress herself in her dried clothes. She took Matt's hand, feeling unbelievably relaxed and foolishly euphoric, and followed him down the stairs.

When they reached the bottom, Matt cast a sidelong glance at his Harley. "You like motorcycles?" he asked Lizabeth.

She didn't want to be insulting, but she liked motorcycles almost as much as she liked tattoos, fat black cigars, and poisonous spiders. "I don't know very much about motorcycles," she said.

He dragged her into the living room. "This is a Harley Sportster. 900cc's. It's a honey, isn't it? It can do everything but bake brownies."

She struggled to find something nice to say about it. "It's very . . . shiny."

"Yeah. That's because I keep her indoors. I used to do some dirt-bike racing when I was first out of the Navy. After I broke my leg for the third time I decided to quit the circuit."

"Is this a dirt bike?"

He grinned down at her. "No. A dirt bike is smaller. The tires are a lot more narrow. This baby is a hog."

Lizabeth nodded. Obviously, if you were a motorcycle it was complimentary to be called a hog.

"You're trying to be polite, but I can see you're not into internal combustion," Matt said. "Bet you've never even ridden on one of these."

"Well, no . . ."

He strapped the gym bag to the back of the seat, handed Lizabeth a big black helmet, and straddled the bike. "Open the front door for me. I'll take you for a ride."

Lizabeth clutched the helmet to her chest and took a step backward. "That's not necessary. It's nice of you to offer, but . . ."

The smile was full of pure little-boy charm. "Come on. You're really going to like this. This is going to be great." He jump-started the big black bike. The motor kicked in and rumbled through the house like thunder. Windows rattled, glasses danced across the kitchen counter, and Lizabeth felt the vibration through the soles of her shoes. "Riding a Harley's the next best thing to good sex," Matt said, hand-revving the engine.

Lizabeth pressed her lips together. She didn't want to miss "the next best thing to good sex," but the thought of riding hell-bent on Matt's Harley made her mouth go dry. She grimly followed him out the door and down the sidewalk to the curb. He patted the seat behind him and smiled.

"Macho garbage," Lizabeth said.

The smile broadened. "Without a shadow of a doubt."

She settled herself on the padded seat, cautiously searched for a place for her feet to rest, and tentatively clutched at his waist. "You have to be careful with me," she said. "I'm a motherrrrrrr!" Her fingers locked onto his shirt, her knuckles went instantly white, and her words were lost in the wind and the roar of the engine as the bike laid rubber and wheeled away from the curb.

Six

Jason was the first to reach the bike when it pulled into the driveway. "Oh man, this is so cool. I hope Noogie Newsome's watching from across the street. He thinks he's so hot because his brother got a scooter. Man, this baby could blast that stupid scooter right off the road."

Lizabeth could barely see her son through the bugs splattered on her Plexiglas visor. She carefully put one foot on the ground and tried to breathe. It was probably the first breath she'd had since leaving Matt's town house, she thought. She reached for the helmet and realized her hands were shaking. It had felt so *fast*. All wind and noise and power.

Matt cut the engine and felt the body go limp behind him. He turned to look over his shoulder and saw that Lizabeth's eyes were huge, her face ashen, her breathing coming in shallow gasps. He set the kickstand and slid off the bike, cursing himself for not checking on her sooner. He put his hands to her waist, pulled her to her feet, and removed her helmet. "You're all right. You're just hyperventilating. Take a deep breath." He massaged her shoulders and the base of her neck. "Try to relax."

Lizabeth nodded, unable to speak. She couldn't remember ever having been so terrified . . . and so exhilarated. She cupped her hands over her nose and mouth and made an effort to slow her breathing.

Matt gently stroked the wet ringlets away from her damp forehead. "Lizabeth," he said, "you have a ways to go before you get those fairy wings."

She patted his chest with her hand. "I'm sure you'll help me."

"I'm trying."

Jason had scrambled onto the bike. "Vrooom, vrooom, vrooom," he said. "I'm gonna get one of these when I grow up. I'm gonna start saving my money."

Lizabeth looked at her son and winced. She didn't want him aspiring to own a motorcycle. She didn't necessarily care if he went to an Ivy League college, and she certainly didn't want him to be as career-obsessed as Paul, but she did have minimum expectations for him. And she didn't consider a fixation with motorcycles to be a step in the right direction. She reluctantly admitted she had a problem. She'd fallen in love with a man who wasn't her idea of a perfect role model for her sons. He was fine as a friend of the family, but what sort of a father would he be, riding around on his motorcycle, getting lewd messages tattooed on his arm.

"C'mon, squirt," Matt said, tucking Jason under his arm. "Let's go inside and look in the oven so I can decide if I want to stay for supper."

Elsie stood on the porch steps. "What's all the racket about? Holy cow, is that a hog in the driveway?"

"It's Matt's," Jason said. "Isn't it awesome?"

"Yep," Elsie said. "It's awesome all right. Nothing like a hog to liven a place up."

Matt gave Elsie a kiss on the cheek. "Play your cards right, and I might take you for a ride after supper."

Lizabeth turned, took one last glance at the Harley, and gave an involuntary shiver. Yes sir, Lizabeth, she thought, you're in way over your head.

Lizabeth cracked her knuckles and resumed her pacing. The bedroom floor was cool under her bare feet, her white cotton gown with the little blue roses billowed around her legs as she walked, and her ears stayed alert for sounds drifting through her open window. It was two o'clock and overcast and the backyard seemed unusually dark. The outside lights hadn't been turned on, and there were no lights shining inside the Victorian house. Even the small night-lights had been extinguished. Elsie and Matt didn't want to scare the flasher off. "It's not fair," Lizabeth said. "It's two against one. And that poor flasher doesn't even have any clothes on." In her mind that gave him some sort of disadvantage, as if he couldn't think as well, or run as fast, because he was nude.

Elsie had dragged the rocking chair into the kitchen. She'd positioned it in front of the back door and left the door ajar so she could hear the slightest sound coming from the yard. She'd been sitting there, in the dark, for almost three hours and she was sound asleep. Her hands were folded, at rest on her stomach, her mouth had dropped open, and her head tilted crazily to one side. Matt sat at the kitchen table, his arms crossed in front of him on the table, his head resting on his arms. His eyelids drooped shut. His breathing was slow and regular. A short nap wouldn't hurt, he decided. He was a light sleeper. He would hear the flasher when he came into the yard.

A stone hit Lizabeth's window. It was a small stone, and the sound it made was so slight it was barely audible. Lizabeth felt her heart jump in her chest. She stood absolutely still, her hands pressed to her mouth, the pulse thumping in her throat. She didn't want anyone to get hurt. Not Matt, not Elsie, not the flasher. She moved to the window and was caught in the beam of the flashlight. Lord, why didn't he just stop. Why didn't he put his clothes on and take up bowling or something. It was almost as if he wanted to get caught. Lizabeth leaned into the window. "Get out of here!" she hissed in her loudest possible whisper.

"What?"

"Get out of here! There's a man in my kitchen who's going to break every bone in your body!"

Matt woke up at the sound of Lizabeth's voice. The kitchen was black as pitch, but Matt was out of his chair and across the room in three strides. The back door was half open and Matt saw the streak of light blink off. He reached for the door and slammed into the rocking chair, dumping Elsie onto the floor.

"What the devil's going on?" Elsie said, coming awake. "Don't anybody get near me. I know judo. I got Mace."

Matt turned the lights on, grabbed Elsie by the elbow, and pulled her to her feet.

Lizabeth came flying down the stairs. "What was that crash?"

"Land sakes, there he goes!" Elsie shouted. "Hey, you damn pervert, you're in trouble now! Matt's gonna break every bone in your naked body!"

The flasher ran across the yard, with Matt in pursuit. Matt dove at the man, catching him by the ankle, propelling them both facedown into the dirt. Ferguson bounded from the open kitchen door and pounced on Matt. The swearing was loud and creative while the dog snuffled into Matt's pockets and the flasher squirmed loose.

"Ferguson!" Lizabeth had him by the collar, but she couldn't get the dog off Matt. "Matt, do you have food in your pockets?"

"M&M's!" he grunted out.

Lizabeth turned the pockets inside out, spilling the candy onto the ground. She looked up in time to see the flasher jump on the Harley. The engine caught and the Harley roared out of the driveway.

"If that don't beat all," Elsie said. "That slimeball

stole your bike. Well, he's not going to get away with this. I got my keys in my pocket. I'll run him down in my Caddy."

Lizabeth ran after her. "I don't think this is a good idea."

"Nonsense," Elsie said, sliding behind the wheel. "I've been on these high-speed chases before. I know what I'm doing."

Matt jumped into the passenger side just as Elsie gunned the engine. Lizabeth and Ferguson climbed into the back and the Cadillac peeled out of the driveway and barreled down the road after the flasher.

Matt braced his arms against the dash. "Elsie, don't you think you're going a little fast? Maybe you should pull over and let me drive."

"No way," Elsie said. "We'll lose him. Besides, I got perfect control over this car." The Cadillac took a corner on a skid and swayed from side to side before finding equilibrium.

"Need new shocks," Elsie shouted over the roar of the V-8 engine. "These ones got mushy on me."

"He's turning down High Street," Matt said.

Elsie grunted and jerked the wheel of the Cadillac. The car jumped the curb and cut across Elmo Nielson's front lawn. "Shortcut," Elsie said. "Won't hurt nothing. Elmo can't grow grass here anyway. Too much shade."

The Cadillac closed in on the flasher, and Lizabeth could see the man's tie flapping over his shoulder and the paper-bag mask rippling with the wind. Flashing lights reflected in the rearview mirror. "Omigod," Lizabeth said, "we've picked up a police cruiser."

The Harley turned into Vinnie Mazerelli's driveway and, without even so much as a backward glance, the flasher cut through Vinnie's yard and disappeared from view.

Elsie stomped on the brake. "Doggone!"

Lizabeth and Ferguson slid off the seat, and the black-and-white cruiser slammed into the back of the Cadillac.

Elsie gave a disgusted sigh. "Wouldn't you think they could teach them cops how to drive?"

Matt rolled his eyes and got out of the car. "Howdy," he said to Officers Dooley and Schmidt.

Dooley nodded. "I don't suppose I have to ask who was driving the Cadillac."

"Don't suppose you do," Matt said.

"And I guess the naked guy slapping leather on the Harley was the flasher?"

"Yup."

Dooley shifted his attention to the squad car. The entire front end was smashed. Both headlights were broken, steam escaped from a cracked radiator, and the bumper was lying on the road. The Cadillac didn't have a scratch.

"You guys got a lot of nerve following so close," Elsie said. "Look here what you've done with the taxpayers' money." She patted the Cadillac's rear fender. "I tell you, they don't make cars like they used to. Next time you get yourselves a car, you get a *real* car. Like my Caddy here."

Dooley's left eye twitched. He put a finger to it and pressed his lips together. "It would probably be best if you took her home, now. I'd hate to be charged with police brutality," he said to Matt.

By the time they got home, the Harley had already been returned. It was parked in the driveway, key still in the ignition, just as Matt had left it.

"You see," Lizabeth said, "he isn't such a bad guy. He even brought your bike back."

The sun broke over the horizon with barely a whimper as Bob the Cat sat on the back stoop cleaning his front feet, pretending nonchalance while keeping an alert ear for the sound of familiar feet treading across the kitchen floor. It was six-thirty and Lizabeth felt raw-eyed from lack of sleep. She quietly crept down the stairs and smiled at the sight of Matt stretched out on the couch in a tangle of sheets. He was fully dressed and looked mildly uncomfortable. He slept on his back with his arm flung over his head, and even in the dim light of dawn the red stubble on his chin was distinctly visible. Lizabeth stood beside the couch and watched him. His breathing was even, like a child's, she thought. But that was where the similarity stopped. There was nothing childlike about the lean planes of his face or the fierce slash of blond eyebrow. His large frame dwarfed the couch and charged the room with virility and latent energy. She wondered if the latter was real or imagined. Her perspective was hardly impartial. She touched his shoulder. "Matt."

The thick, curly blond lashes fluttered open, and he stared at Lizabeth with unfocused eyes. "I'm not in my bed," he said. "Am I in yours?"

"No. You're on my couch."

"Oh yeah. Now I remember. I was having this awful nightmare that I was chasing the flasher and Ferguson attacked me. And then the flasher stole my motorcycle because I stupidly left the key in the ignition. Then we went on this bizarre ride with Elsie . . ."

"It's all true."

He closed his eyes and groaned. "I'm going to kill myself. I'm a failure. I let a potbellied, out-of-shape pervert get away from me. You aren't going to tell the guys at work about this, are you?"

"Speaking of the guys at work . . . it's after six."

"Oh hell, I have a building inspector coming at seven." He swung his legs over the side of the couch and ran a hand through his hair. "I have a stack of forms to fill out before he arrives."

"Will they take long to fill out?"

"No. It's finding them that's going to be the problem." He shuffled into his shoes and swung an arm around her shoulders. "I'll give you a raise if you'll help me look for the forms."

Three hours later Lizabeth was still sifting through papers on Matt's desk. She'd found a half-eaten salami sub, a red wool sock, notice that the lease on his town house was due to expire, and a month-old unopened letter with the return address of J. Hallahan, Scranton, Pennsylvania, but she hadn't found the appropriate forms for the building inspector. She pushed her chair back when Matt stomped down the basement stairs. "You need help," she said. "You're in big trouble with this paperwork."

He slouched in a battered oak captain's chair, stretching his long legs in front of him. "I know. Did you find the forms?"

She shook her head. "No. But they're going to evict you from your town house if you don't do something immediately. And I found this letter." She slid the white envelope from J. Hallahan across the top of the desk.

Matt looked at it and slid it back to her. "Throw it away."

"Aren't you going to open it?"

"It's nothing important."

Lizabeth leaned forward, resting her elbows on the desk. "It's from a relative. Did you read the return address? It's from a J. Hallahan."

"I know who it's from."

"Ah-hah." She tapped her index finger on the envelope. It seemed to her that copulation carried some privileges—such as the right to be nosy. "So, who's this J. Hallahan?"

"He's my father."

Lizabeth's eyebrows shot up in silent question.

"It's a request for money, and I've already sent some. There's no reason to open the envelope. The letters are always the same." He should tell her about it, he thought, but he hated dragging all those skeletons out of the closet. He didn't want to seem pitiable in her eyes. And he didn't want to seem callous. And he knew if he told her he would appear to be both. When he was eighteen he'd literally run away from his past. In some ways he was still running. Always would be. He could see she was concerned about the contents of the letter, so he took it from her, opened it, and glanced over his father's almost unreadable scrawl. His mouth curved into the tight, crooked smile he reserved for those times when he managed to find some wry humor in distasteful situations. "No surprises here," he said, handing the letter to her so she could read it for herself. "Someday we'll sit down with a bottle of wine and tell each other all our grim family secrets. Fortunately, I haven't got the time to do it right now." He stood with his hands on his hips, his brows drawn together in a scowl. "Damn, I wish we could find those forms." His eyes swept over the desk, the file cabinets, the cases of cola stacked on the floor. A guilty smile spread across his face. "I remember! It was raining when I brought the forms back from the municipal building." He went to the open area behind the stairwell, picked up a pair of rubber boots caked with dried mud, and under the boots he found the forms. "I didn't want to get the floor dirty," he explained, wiping at the brown smudges.

Lizabeth bit her lower lip and considered Matthew Hallahan's husband potential. He was sensitive, sexy, and he had a decent income, she decided—but he'd be hell to housebreak. She took the forms from him and smoothed them out on the desktop. "Want me to have a go at this?"

"That'd be great." He noticed the neat piles of papers on the desk. She'd cleaned up the dried splotches where he'd spilled coffee and chicken noodle soup, and she'd gotten the smear of roofing tar off the telephone. The salami sub had been removed from his out box, and had been replaced with a batch of stamped, unsealed envelopes.

Lizabeth gestured to the envelopes. "There were a few things I felt comfortable handling, but you'd better check everything just to make sure. I've tried to divide the rest up into categories. Bills, bids, contracts. I've filed the catalogs and advertisements."

She'd shut off the air-conditioning and opened the sliding patio door, letting the moist morning air pour into the basement. Her hair had begun to curl in ringlets that pressed against her temples and straggled over her forehead, and her face was alive with a sense of accomplishment. Matt watched her push the hair back from her face, and felt himself go breathless. Every movement she made excited him, every part of her seemed perfect, exquisite. He wanted to reach out and tangle his hand in her hair. He wanted to kiss the spot of downy-soft skin in front of her earlobe. He wanted to hear the little catch in her throat that meant passion had caught her by surprise, had overwhelmed her, had rushed through her like a flash fire. Another time, he told himself. He wasn't in the mood to start something he couldn't finish. Three hours of sleep had left him with a short fuse. He was trying to impress the lady with his compassion and sensitivity. So he struggled to keep up the casual attitude they normally fell into during work hours.

She was the sort of woman who always rose to a challenge, he thought. And she took pride in a job well done. He liked that in a person. He didn't have a bunch of fancy degrees behind his name, but he knew everything there was to know about building houses. He could figure out a mortgage payment faster than a calculator. And he knew about people. He knew talent when he saw it, and he knew he needed Lizabeth in the office almost as badly as he needed her in his life. "Lizabeth, you've just been promoted to General Office Manager. You're going to like this job. It pays twice as much as your old one."

"Can you afford to do that?"

Matt glanced down at the wrinkled forms on the desk. "I can't afford not to. I'm sinking. I build beautiful houses, but I'm an unorganized slob."

It was the truth, Lizabeth thought. He was a slob, and he was sinking. From what she'd seen this morning, bills were going unpaid through negligence, several bids had expired, and food poisoning had to be a constant danger. "Do I work the same hours?"

"You work whatever hours you want. If you can get the job done in three hours and want to go home, that's fine by me. I'll pay you for a full day anyway." And she would be rested by evening, he thought. He had plans for her evenings.

She was still working at five-thirty. "I'm almost done," she said, running her finger down a column of numbers. "I've made out tomorrow's payroll checks, and I think I've got your accounting system figured out. It's no wonder you couldn't run this office while you were building houses. Five years ago, when you and Frank went into business for yourselves, you were building one house at a time, and the paperwork was manageable. You're now building three houses on this site, and you have a fifteen-acre parcel of land seven miles south of here that you're having partially cleared for future development. You've expanded your business, but you haven't expanded your support staff. For starters, I think you need a professional accountant. And I think you need to upgrade your office equipment."

"I know. Frank and I had been talking about it, and then he broke his hip, and I didn't have time to look into any of that stuff. Maybe you could do it for me. Find us an accountant, and buy whatever you think we need." He closed the ledger she was studying. "Right now, we need to go home. You know how Elsie hates people being late for dinner. If I don't get you home by six she won't feed me."

Lizabeth stood and stretched and realized they'd driven to work on the Harley. That meant they were going to have to go home on the Harley. Unless she chickened out and walked. The thought prompted a small groan that was caught and squelched midway in her throat. She wasn't sure what the groan represented. Fear? Excitement? Embarrassment? She followed Matt up the stairs and said a silent prayer that a miracle would happen and they could sneak into her driveway without anyone noticing. If she was going to hyperventilate, she'd prefer to do it with some privacy.

"Lord, Lizabeth," Matt said, "you look like you're going to keel over, and you haven't even gotten on the bike yet." He massaged the back of her neck. "You have to relax."

"I'm relaxed," Lizabeth said.

"Honey, you're not breathing. Listen, we could walk. Or I could zip on home and come back for you in the truck." He felt her spine stiffen, felt determination push aside fear. She was a fighter. She wasn't a woman who gave in to weakness. Hawkins blood, Elsie would say. And she might be right. The thought brought a smile to his lips.

"What's so funny?"

"I was just thinking that you and Elsie are a lot alike."

"Omigod."

Ten minutes later they pulled into Lizabeth's driveway, and a silver Lincoln pulled up behind them. Matt and Lizabeth got off the bike, removed their helmets and watched Paul Kane emerge from his air-conditioned car. His hair was dark, peppered with gray at the temples. His features were classic all-American and as bland as white bread. He was wearing a gray pin-striped, summer-wool, custom-tailored suit, starched pinpoint oxford-cloth cotton shirt, burgundy silk foulard tie. The first expression to register on his face was surprise, quickly followed by undisguised disgust.

"My ex-husband," Lizabeth said.

Matt squinted at him. "It's eighty-five in the shade. How does he manage to look like that?"

"Paul Kane's pants wouldn't dare wrinkle."

So far Matt hadn't liked anything he'd heard about Paul Kane, and now that he saw him he liked him even less. He especially didn't like the way he was looking at Lizabeth. "Suppose I punch him in the nose."

"I don't think that's necessary. Seeing the mother

of his children on the back of a motorcycle had to be the equivalent of a good punch in the gut."

Matt slid a protective arm around her shoulders. "Sorry he caught you rolling in on my Harley. Are you embarrassed?"

Lizabeth tipped her head back and laughed. "Are you kidding? This Harley has class! It's a hog. I never really appreciated it until I saw the look on Paul's face."

"He was horrified," Matt said.

"Mmmm," Lizabeth mused. "I probably looked like that the first time I saw your Harley sitting in your living room. But I'm better now," she added. "I can run across a board in the rain, and I can almost have fun on a motorcycle."

She closed the gap between the two men and extended her hand. "Nice to see you again, Paul." He gave her the required hand squeeze and cast a glance at the house. He withheld comment, but the glance was enough. Five years ago she would have been devastated by that dismissal, Lizabeth thought. Today she found it amusing, maybe even satisfying. Her house didn't measure up to Paul Kane's standards and to her that seemed to be a step in the right direction. Paul Kane was a snob, a stuffed shirt, a shallow person. And to quote Elsie, he was a horse's behind.

"Seems to be a family-oriented neighborhood," Paul said. "I imagine you feel comfortable here."

"It's perfect," Lizabeth said. "The boys have lots of friends. They can walk to school, and I can walk to work."

Concern flicked across Kane's brow. "What sort of job do you have that you can walk to work?"

His mouth tightened. "You're not a domestic, are you?"

"No," Lizabeth said, "I'm a carpenter. Actually, I suppose I'm not a carpenter anymore. I just got a promotion."

"Wonderful. What were you promoted to? Backhoe driver?"

"Office manager," Lizabeth said, enjoying the moment, knowing Paul wouldn't think any more of office manager than backhoe driver. "And this is my boss, Matt Hallahan."

The two men measured each other. When it became obvious neither was going to observe the usual amenity of a polite handshake, Lizabeth took over. "Elsie will be serving dinner in a few minutes." She turned to Paul. "Would you like to join us? It will give you a chance to say hello to the boys."

Color suddenly stained his cheeks. "Elsie's here? Crazy Elsie Hawkins? The woman who talks to pigeons?"

Lizabeth smiled. This was getting better and better. "Elsie's spending the summer with us. I needed a baby-sitter for Billy and Jason."

"I suppose Lizzie Borden was your first choice."

"Very funny," Lizabeth said. "I'm going to tell Elsie you said that, and she'll make you eat pork chop fat."

Elsie met them on the front porch. "You come all the way up from Virginia just so you could mooch a pork chop?" she said to Paul.

Paul made a strangled sound in the back of his throat. "Nice to see you again, Elsie."

"He wants something," Elsie said to Lizabeth

when they were alone in the kitchen. "The man's a taker. Never could understand why you married him. The first time I laid eyes on him I thought he was a pig's patoot."

Lizabeth took the buttermilk biscuits from the oven and dumped them into a basket lined with a white linen napkin. She and the boys had lived alone for over a year now, and Paul had called only a handful of times. He'd sent their Christmas presents UPS and completely missed Jason's birthday. Lizabeth had to agree with Elsie. There was no possibility that this was simply a friendly visit. She filled a big bowl with mashed potatoes that had been warming on the stove and filled another bowl with steamed green beans. She took the pork chops and cooked apple rings from the oven and arranged them on a ceramic platter. Ferguson quietly inched his way up behind her and grabbed a pork chop.

"Damn dog!" Elsie shouted, smacking Ferguson on the top of his head with her wooden spoon. Ferguson opened his mouth in surprise, and the pork chop fell onto the linoleum floor. Elsie picked the pork chop up and brushed it off. "It's okay," she said, carefully setting it apart from the others. "We'll give it to Paul."

Matt might have cheered up some over dinner if he'd known Paul was eating dog drool. As it was he was having a difficult time dealing with the emotions Paul Kane triggered in him. He was overwhelmed with protective instincts and powerless to act on them. His anger simmered as he watched two of the most gregarious children he'd ever met turn excruciatingly shy. Jason and Billy hadn't mumbled more than three words throughout the entire meal. They kept their eyes on their plates, fiddling with their meat and pushing their beans into their mashed potatoes. Matt understood the sudden personality shift. He knew what it was like to be ignored by your father. And he knew all the manifestations of rejection: denial, animosity, self-doubt. People like Paul Kane didn't deserve to have terrific kids like Billy and Jason, and Billy and Jason didn't deserve to have a father like Paul Kane. Matt almost felt sorry for Kane. The man had to be a total imbecile to have let Lizabeth, Jason, and Billy walk out of his life. A mistake he didn't intend to make, Matt thought. He wanted to give them all the love he'd never received. All the support. All the understanding. He wanted to teach the boys to paddle a canoe, and he wanted to buy them ice-cream cones on hot summer nights, and he wanted to be there when they split their lips trying to do wheelies on their dirt bikes.

The evening was growing painful for Lizabeth as well. The earlier joy at shocking her ex-husband had turned to despair as she watched her sons struggle through the meal. She'd forgotten how tongue-tied they became when they were with their dad. She shouldn't have invited him to dinner, but she'd honestly hoped for a warm reunion. Actually, Paul wasn't behaving badly, she thought. He was being the perfect politician, making innocuous dinner conversation, smiling at the appropriate moments, easing around Elsie's occasional barbs. It was the sort of performance that had first piqued her interest in him. He could be gracious and charming when he wanted, and fool that she was, she had married him, not realizing that the interest in others was feigned and the kindness self-serving. Paul Kane was an entirely selfish man.

Billy and Jason Kane knew all this. And it didn't matter. He was their dad, and they waited like street urchins, silently begging for crumbs of affection and acceptance.

"Well, what have you accomplished this summer?" Paul asked Jason.

Jason looked at his father with wide eyes. At age eight he still had a soft, baby's mouth. The mouth opened, but no words emerged. He blinked once and held tightly to his fork. "Nothin'," he finally whispered.

"Surely you've done something?"

"No sir."

Paul Kane looked pleased. "I think you'll find the next two weeks a nice change of pace then. For the next two weeks you'll have lots of interesting things to do."

Lizabeth leaned forward slightly. "What are you talking about?"

"Surely you haven't forgotten. These are my two weeks with the boys. It was very clearly spelled out in the divorce agreement."

Panic prickled at the nape of Lizabeth's neck and expanded in her chest, making it difficult to breathe. "But you've never called! You've never mentioned it. You've never shown any desire to spend time with them . . ."

"I've been busy," Paul said, a sly little cat's smile playing over his face.

Billy coolly stared at his father. "What will we do with you?"

"You'll come live in my house, of course. I've made arrangements for you to have tennis and swim lessons at the club."

"I guess that would be okay," Billy said. "It's just for two weeks, isn't it?"

Jason bit into his lower lip. "Can I bring my bear?"

Paul looked to Lizabeth. "His bear?"

"You remember, the fuzzy brown teddy bear he takes to bed. Woobie."

"You won't be needing Woobie," Paul said to Jason. "You'll have better things to occupy your mind."

Jason pressed his lips together and scowled. "I'm not going without Woobie."

Paul shot Lizabeth a look that said his suspicions had been confirmed. She was a total failure as a mother.

"Of course you can take Woobie," Elsie said. "And I'll take care of him for you when you go off to them fancy tennis lessons."

Kane raised his eyebrows. "Excuse me?"

"Don't worry about it," Elsie said. "I'm not charging Lizabeth anything for being nursemaid and I won't charge you neither."

"I don't need a nursemaid . . ."

"Of course you need a nursemaid. An eight-year-old needs constant supervision. You gonna watch him twenty-four hours a day so he don't nail your shoes to the floor? And more than that, you're not taking these kids out of the house without me. I agreed to take care of them for the summer and that's what I aim to do."

"Suppose I refuse to take you."

Elsie narrowed her eyes. "Then I get in my Caddy, and I drive to that ritzy house you got in Virginia, and I sit on the lawn until the police come to take me away. I imagine that'll be pretty newsworthy. If I sit on that lawn long enough I might make *Good Morning America*."

Kane considered it for a moment. "I suppose a live-in baby-sitter wouldn't be a bad idea."

Elsie plunked a fresh-baked apple pie on the table. "You help yourself to some pie, and I'll get us all packed up."

Seven

Lizabeth sat on her front porch and watched the sun set behind Noogie Newsome's house. She cast a disparaging glance at the tent caterpillars in the Newsomes' crab-apple tree and clucked her tongue at the rusted antenna that halfheartedly clung to the Newsomes' chimney. "Sunsets aren't what they used to be," she said with a sigh.

Matt cocked an eyebrow. "What did they used to be?"

"Pretty. They used to be pretty." She hunched forward, elbows on knees, chin resting on her hands. "Who wants to see the sun setting behind the Newsomes' ugly old TV antenna?"

"Honey, the sun always sets behind the Newsomes' TV antenna."

"Yes, but I never had time to watch it set before. I never realized how ugly it was."

Matt patted her on the knee and continued to scratch the top of Ferguson's head.

"And it's boring in this neighborhood. People grow grass as an intellectual pursuit," Lizabeth said.

"It's not such a bad neighborhood."

"Sure, it's fine if you have kids and they keep you busy. Then you don't have time to be grossed out by lawn fungus."

"Lizabeth, the kids have only been gone for a half hour."

"You think they'll be okay?"

It was the four hundredth time she'd asked that since Paul had left with Jason and Billy. Matt answered it just as he always did. "They'll be fine. Elsie's with them."

"I suppose you're right," she said morosely. She stared at the Newsomes' chimney, and a tear squeezed out of her eye and trickled down her cheek. "I hate that damn TV antenna."

Matt wiped the tear away and gathered her to him. "We need to take your mind off this antenna stuff. We need recreation."

"I don't want to leave the house," Lizabeth said softly. "Elsie said she'd call when they got to Richmond."

"Your answering machine will take the message."

"I don't have an answering machine."

"Oh. Well then, how about if we rent a movie for the VCR?"

"I don't have a VCR."

Ferguson sunk his teeth into Matt's shirtsleeve and gave it a yank. Matt stuck his finger through the hole Ferguson had made and scowled. "Forget it. I'm not scratching your head anymore."

"It's my fault," Lizabeth said. "He always gets grumpy when I get grumpy. He's very sensitive."

Matt thought Ferguson was about as sensitive as a brick. "All right, you and Ferguson stay here, and I'll see what I can do about the evening's entertainment."

"No mud wrestlers, please."

He left on the motorcycle, but he returned in the truck. Lizabeth looked at the boxes and quilted bundles in the back of the pickup. "What is all this? It looks like laundry."

"It's stuff from my house. I figure it'll get more use over here."

She grabbed a box and trailed after him. He'd brought a VCR, a telephone answering machine, his popcorn popper, two boxes of movies, a box full of junk food, a Monopoly game that looked like it had been run over by a semi, a huge jug of red wine, and a small paper bag that Lizabeth discovered contained three packages of condoms—thirty-six in all.

Matt looked at his cache of goodies. "This should keep us busy."

Lizabeth held the little bag between thumb and forefinger. "Thirty-six?"

"You think I overestimated?"

"You weren't planning on using them all tonight, were you?"

"I must look like Super Stud. The check-out lady asked me the same thing." He carried the VCR into the living room and hooked it up to Lizabeth's television. "I brought some movies I had at home. One box is blood and guts, and the other is general entertainment."

Lizabeth noticed the general-entertainment box was much smaller than the blood-and-guts box. She hated violence, and, as a mother, felt a strong obligation to discourage its glorification. She didn't want murder and mayhem to seem like everyday events to her children. "Matt, suppose we eventually got married, and Jason wanted to watch something from the blood-and-guts box?"

"I'd say no. Then he'd probably whine and cry and say Noogie Newsome got to watch blood-and-guts movies, and if blood-and-guts movies were so bad then why did I have a whole big box of them?"

"Would that change your mind about letting him watch blood and guts?"

"No, but I'd feel like a real crumb."

"Suppose Jason wanted a tattoo?"

"No tattoos. Tattoos are dumb. I don't want my son having pierced ears either." He carted the popcorn maker into the kitchen and took a bag of popcorn out of the junk-food box.

Lizabeth smiled to herself. She'd been worried about nothing. He had answered all the questions correctly. "And motorcycles! What if your son wanted a motorcycle?"

"Man, that would be great! We could go biking together."

She dropped a chunk of butter into a saucepan and put the pan on the stove. There were lots worse things than motorcycles, she told herself. Drugs, rabid bats, cholera. And it wasn't as if she and Matt were getting married tomorrow. They were merely lovers, and lovers were allowed some eccentricities. She rolled her eyes. What a bunch of baloney. Her feelings for Matt were strong and deep. The thought of having a brief romance with him held absolutely no appeal. They weren't merely lovers. They were in love, and they were tiptoeing around marriage. At least she was tiptoeing, Lizabeth thought. Matt was stomping straight ahead. Matt could afford to stomp straight ahead. He didn't have two children to consider.

A lump suddenly formed in her throat and her vision blurred. She missed Jason and Billy. They'd been the focal point of her life for ten years and she felt bereft without them. Boy, is this ever dumb, she thought. I'm really being a dope. The lump got larger.

Matt recognized the look of utter despair and guessed at its origin. He wrapped her in his arms and kissed her forehead. "They're going to be fine," he murmured, praying she didn't burst into tears, because he'd probably cry right along with her. He didn't completely understand this business of motherhood, but he was beginning to feel the power of it. And he was relieved to discover his own capacity for love. There had been a lot of years when he wondered if he had the emotional makeup to be a father and husband. There'd been a lot of years when he'd worried about duplicating his own childhood. He now knew it had been nonsense. He was his own person. Different from his parents. His mistakes would be different, he thought ruefully. "Motherhood is hell, isn't it?"

She sniffed and tried to smile. "I'm being silly."

He hugged her closer. "I don't think you're silly. You love your kids. I think that's terrific."

"It's more than that." She took the melted butter from the stove and set it on a hot pad. "My kids will survive two weeks with Paul. Elsie will shore up their trampled egos. They'll learn how to swim and play tennis. The problem is me. I don't know how to stop being a mother. My children are gone, and I don't know how to entertain myself. This is a terrific opportunity for us to be alone and have some fun together, and all I can do is complain about the Newsomes' TV antenna."

Matt poured the butter over the popcorn. "You're being too hard on yourself. You just need some time to adjust. We're going to sit down and watch a movie, and I bet by the time the movie's over we'll be having fun together."

He was right. By the time the movie was over they'd reduced the number of items in the little drugstore bag to thirty-four.

Lizabeth came awake slowly, at first knowing only that she was hot and uncomfortable. Her bedroom window was wide open but the curtains hung sentinel-straight in the still air. Her hair stuck to the nape of her neck and perspiration pooled between her breasts. Matt was sprawled on top of her, a heavy leg thrown over hers, a possessive arm pinning her to the damp sheet. She tried to wriggle free, but the arm tightened. This would be wonderful at twenty degrees below zero, she thought, but tonight it was oppressive. Not only was he sweating on her, but something was poking into her side. She quickly identified the offending object. "Omigod," she giggled. "Not again!"

He mumbled in his sleep and half opened his eyes. "Hot."

Lizabeth gasped as his large hand roamed across her breast in sensuous exploration. Was he kidding? It had to be a hundred and forty degrees in the bedroom. It was the middle of the night, and she wasn't even sure if he was awake.

He pressed himself hard against her hip and groaned. "Is this a dream?" Then he answered himself. "No. Dreams don't perspire." He kissed her shoulder and moved his hand down her rib cage, across her belly, and lower.

A minute ago she didn't think she could get any warmer, but she'd been wrong! Liquid fire roiled through her with each stroke of his thumb. She swore at him for waking her up with his overheated body, and she swore at him for having such clever fingers.

"Do you like it?" he asked.

Yes, she liked it. She liked the way he took possession of her, and she liked her newfound capacity for passion. She gloried in her own sensuality, clenching her teeth and grabbing handfuls of the sheet as desire surged so strong under his hand it became almost unbearable. He slid between her legs and kissed her. The kiss was sweet and hard. Love and passion. He continued to kiss her while he entered. He knew his way now. He knew the rhythm she liked. Knew how to drive her wild. And he knew how to satisfy her. There was a moment when time stood still, when they hovered at the brink, staring into each other's eyes. It was only a moment, and then they skittered off into the dark, pulsating void of sexual release.

They clung to each other for a long time afterward, too sated, too exhausted to care about damp sheets and record-breaking temperatures. A stone flicked at the window, but they didn't hear it over their own heartbeats. Another stone hit, and Lizabeth opened her eyes.

Maybe it was her imagination, she thought. He couldn't possibly be back. Not after last night!

The flashlight beam swept across her empty window. It was followed by several more stones.

Matt growled. "Ignore him," he said. "Elsie and the boys are gone. For all I care, he can stand naked in your backyard until he drops dead from starvation."

There was a period of silence and then another flurry of stones.

Lizabeth sighed. "He's persistent."

"An admirable quality, but he'll have to flash himself tonight. I'm not getting out of this bed and neither are you."

The light made a second pass over, followed by scuffling sounds. Lizabeth and Matt lay perfectly still, pretending disinterest, but listening intently. They heard the flasher give a small grunt right before a size-ten docksider came crashing through the top half of the bedroom window.

Matt bolted out of bed. "That's it! That's the end of the line. No more Mister Nice Guy." He flew out of the room and thundered down the stairs.

Lizabeth followed after him, realized she was naked, and ran back for her robe and slippers.

From the upstairs hall window she caught a glimpse of a naked man streaking across her lawn. Suddenly there was a lot of shouting. Red and blue flashing lights reflected off the stand of pine trees. And lights blinked on all over the neighborhood. Lizabeth raced through the house and out the back door. The police had a man on the ground and neighbors were converging on her yard from all directions.

"We've got him," Officer Schmidt said. "We didn't have anything better to do tonight, so we thought we'd stake out your yard, and it paid off!" The naked man was facedown in the dirt and Schmidt's knee was square in the middle of the man's bare back.

It was pitch-black, without so much as a sliver of a moon, but Lizabeth had enough light to recognize the long, muscular legs stretched out behind Schmidt. "You've done it again, you numskull!" she shouted at Schmidt. "That's not the flasher. That's Matt!"

"Listen, lady, this guy was running through your yard in his birthday suit!"

"Mmmm. Well, I could see where you might make a mistake, but this is Matt. He was chasing the flasher."

Schmidt removed his knee. "Sorry." He looked around nervously. "Where's the old lady? She isn't running around in the buff too, is she?"

Matt stood and dusted himself off, and Lucille Wainstock gasped, and Emma Newsome giggled. Marvin Miller loaned Matt his robe, and Kathy White called Marvin a spoilsport.

"Excuse me," Bette Sliwicky said, "but I don't

understand about this second naked man. Not that I'm complaining, but if he isn't a flasher, why doesn't he have any clothes on?"

Emma Newsome lapsed into a coughing fit.

Just great, Lizabeth thought. Here she was recently divorced with two young children, and she had a naked man spending the night with her. This would do wonderful things for her reputation. At least she wouldn't have to worry about being asked to run for president of the PTA.

"I don't have any clothes on because that's the way I sleep . . . without clothes," Matt said.

"He ran out without thinking," Lizabeth added. "The real flasher threw a shoe and broke my bedroom window, and so Matt jumped out of bed and um . . ." Did she just say that? Did she actually just tell these people Matt was sleeping naked in her bed? She heard the sound of several eyebrows being raised and gave herself a mental kick. Billy and Jason would pay for this. Word was going to get back to them that their mother was a loose woman. She tilted her nose up a fraction of an inch and pasted a smile on her face. "It just occurred to me that, with the possible exception of Officer Schmidt and Officer Dooley, none of you have been introduced to Matt. I'd like you all to meet Matt Hallahan, my husband."

There was a collective moment of silence. "Is this a *new* husband?" Emma Newsome finally asked.

Matt put his arm around Lizabeth and hauled her to his side. "Yup," he said, "I'm brand-new. We just got married yesterday."

"Is that the reason for the barbecue Saturday?"

Emma Newsome asked. "It's sort of a wedding reception. How nice!" She hugged Lizabeth. "I'm so happy for you."

Lucille Wainstock hugged Lizabeth, and so did Bette Sliwicky. Marvin Miller slapped Matt on the back. "You need an extra grill Saturday? I can drag mine over."

"Congratulations," Officer Schmidt said to Matt. "You aren't gonna have to live with Lead Foot, are you?"

"She's just here for the summer."

"If you'll all excuse us," Lizabeth said. "There are things I have to discuss with my husband."

Matt followed her into the house. He closed and locked the kitchen door and tried not to look too pleased over the fact that he was suddenly married. He knew Lizabeth well enough by now to recognize the slight tremor of fury in her voice. Her back was ramrod straight and her eyes snapped at him in the dark kitchen. He had placed her in an awkward situation. He should probably apologize. "Sorry."

"Sorry? *Sorry?* That's all you have to say? Sorry? Of all the stupid, moronic, thoughtless—"

"Yeah, those cops are really dumb, aren't they?"

"Not the cops. *You!* You went charging out of the house with no clothes on. And then, as if that isn't bad enough, you just stood there in front of the whole neighborhood, dusting yourself off."

"Well, what did you expect me to do? Go jumping around like an embarrassed teenager? I didn't see that I had a whole lot of options. And anyway, how come I'm not getting any sympathy for being tackled by the Keystone Kops? Don't you want to know if I skinned my . . . knee?"

The borrowed robe was open, exposing a good six inches of his most vital parts from neck to knees. It was apparent he hadn't skinned anything important, and she was finding it increasingly difficult to remember exactly why she was so angry. "You wouldn't have gotten tackled if you hadn't gone berserk. What about 'ignore him and he'll go away'?"

"The man is a lunatic. He threw a shoe through your window." Damned if women weren't confusing. He'd risked life and limb to protect her from some yuppie pervert, and she was mad at him! He yanked the refrigerator door open and angrily peered inside. He found a small container of leftover potato salad and went in search of a fork.

Lizabeth clenched her fists. "Stop clattering in the silverware when we're having a discussion!"

"I'm hungry. Let me tell you something: Being married to you leaves a lot to be desired."

Lizabeth stepped back as if she'd been slapped. He wasn't the first man to tell her that. Paul had made her constantly aware of her inadequacies as a wife, and years of hurt and insecurity suddenly welled to the surface. She blinked back tears, thankful for the darkness. This time there was a measure of truth in his accusation. Matt hadn't had such a great night either, and she should have been more concerned with his feelings. Somehow that made it all the worse. A feeling of failure came rolling in like fog. It was silent and isolating. And, like fog it swam away from her as she moved forward, but it was always there, obscuring life. Anger, on the other hand, was something she could sink her teeth into. "We're not married!"

"Lizzy, I have a news flash for you. In the eyes of this community, we're about as married as anyone can get."

She smacked the heel of her hand against her forehead. "How could I have been so dumb? Why did I tell all those people you were my husband?"

Matt speared a chunk of potato. "You were a desperate woman, Lizzy. You panicked."

There was a hint of laughter behind his eyes. Damn him, he was in the driver's seat. And he knew it. He held her reputation in the palm of his hand. She tightened the sash on her robe. "I suppose I have a few options."

"You can sell the house and move to Montana."

Lizabeth rolled her eyes.

He set the plastic container on the counter and crossed his arms over his chest. His voice was soft. A whisper in the darkness. "We could actually get married."

Her heart jumped in her chest. Marry him. The possibility shimmered in front of her. It was a great big soap bubble of an idea, and it dredged a giggle up from somewhere deep inside. A lifetime of Matt Hallahan grinning at her over the morning paper. A lifetime of warm sheets, and double dares, and fresh doughnuts from the bakery. He'd protect her from dragons and flashers and hold her close while he slept. And he'd love her long into the night, whispering outrageous suggestions and words of endearment.

Unfortunately, soap bubbles are fragile and short-lived, and Lizabeth needed something that would endure. Her husband would also be father to her children. She couldn't risk another failed marriage, and what it would do to her sons. And then there was still the motorcycle. She put her fingers to her temples, where a dull throb was taking hold.

"Got a headache?"

She nodded. "It's been a long day."

Lizabeth opened her eyes to a sun-drenched room. Matt had crawled in next to her last night, hugging her to him as if his big body could ward away all earthly problems. And to some extent it could. When she was wrapped in his arms, well-being seeped through the layers of self-doubt. This morning the bed was empty next to her, and she felt a stab of panic. He was gone. Could she blame him? She closed her eyes and groaned. Her life was a mess. "Lizabeth," she said, "you screwed up." She looked at the clock and gasped. It was after ten! And someone was knocking on her front door.

Lizabeth wrapped her robe tight around herself and answered the door. "Yes?"

"Blue Star Glass. I'm supposed to fix a window."

He was short and chunky, and he was wearing a blue shirt with *Mike* written over the pocket in red script. She stared at him blank-faced, still half asleep. "You must have the wrong house."

"I don't think so. I got a work order for this address. Very weird, too. Some guy came in first thing this morning, all dressed up in a suit and tie, wearing a paper bag over his head. He said he accidentally broke your bedroom window last night, and he paid me to fix it. Lady, you have some strange friends."

It was close to twelve when Lizabeth got to work. She scanned the street, but she didn't see Matt's truck or bike. Landscapers were laying sod and planting azaleas in the front yard of the colonial. Backhoes were working across the street, excavating basements. The cul-de-sac would be completed by spring. The carpenters would be replaced by mothers and children. The whine of power tools would give way to the drone of televisions and vacuum cleaners. People would be complaining that they couldn't grow grass because Matt had left too many trees. He'd done it purposely so the cul-de-sac would fit in with the older, more established community.

It was quiet and cool in the colonial. Lizabeth stepped into the foyer and listened for the sound of men working. She heard nothing. The house was pretty much done. Next week they would move the office into the house next door, and that's where it would stay until spring. Matt had decided to use the second house as a model rather than sell it immediately. She hesitated at the top of the basement stairs, feeling odd in the empty house, wondering if she was still the office manager. A lot had happened in twenty-four hours, and she wasn't sure how Matt felt about any of it.

A phone rang, and the recorder clicked on. "Matt? Are you there? I know you're there!" Thirty seconds of colorful swearing in a deep, masculine voice. "I hate these damn recorders. I hate talking to a machine. And I hate having people listen to me talk to a machine. I don't know why I bother anyway, because nobody ever calls me the hell back. My number is . . ." The time ran out and the recorder cut off and rewound.

Lizabeth hurried down the stairs and played back the rest of the messages. It was after five when she finally stood and stretched. She hadn't seen Matt all day, but she'd found a terse note taped to the desk saying he'd be at the lawyer's most of the afternoon. Probably trying to see if he could get an annulment from a nonexistent marriage, she thought. She heard the front door open and close. Footsteps overhead going into the kitchen. Her heart skipped a beat. The workmen were all long gone. It was either Matt or a serial murderer. She contemplated sneaking out the patio door.

"Lizabeth?"

It was Matt. And it was too late to sneak away. He stood at the head of the stairs, his body backlit by the kitchen light. He seemed impossibly big, slouched in the doorway. "I was just getting ready to go home," Lizabeth said, sliding past him.

"So was I. And then I realized I had this problem." His voice was weary. "I couldn't figure out where I lived."

He wore a dark pin-striped suit that was perfectly cut to his broad shoulders and slim hips. His white shirt was open at the neck. His tie had been loosened. The slightly pleated slacks clung to his muscular thighs and gracefully fell to a pair of black, Italian leather loafers. He looked more like a CEO than a carpenter. And that's exactly what he is, Lizabeth thought with a jolt. He and Frank Kocen, his hospitalized partner, were the executive officers of Hal-Cen Corporation. It wasn't General Motors, but it was a respectable little construction company, and from what she could see it was growing at a slow but steady pace. They weren't taking any chances. They were building good homes at a reasonable price and reinvesting their profits.

She watched him go to the refrigerator and take out a can of cold beer. She'd never envisioned him in a suit. In fact, she had never thought that he might own one. A five-o'clock shadow was darkening his jaw, whitening his teeth, emphasizing the hard planes of his face. If she'd met him on the street she might not have recognized him at first, but she sure would have given him a second glance. She half expected to see women lined up on the front lawn like cats in heat. He was awesome.

"You're staring," he said.

"I'm not used to seeing you in a suit."

He grunted, oblivious to his own image, and took a swig from the can. "As the company grows, I find myself spending less time on the job site and more time closeted with bankers and lawyers and real estate agents. Especially since Frank broke his hip. It's not something I enjoy. I chose construction because I like the hands-on part of building things."

"When Frank comes back will you be able to retire your suit?"

"Pretty much. As long as you stay in the office. You were right about needing more support staff. Frank and I can't handle it any longer." He finished the beer. "How do you feel about that?"

"I like working in the office."

He wasn't really asking if she liked it. He wanted to know if she was going to stick around. He knew the thought of marrying him gave her a headache. That wasn't an encouraging sign. Last night he'd felt desperate as she curled next to him in bed. He'd only just found her, and he was afraid he'd already lost her. He couldn't even figure out what had gone wrong. One minute they were friends and lovers, and the next thing he knew, she was furious because he'd charged off after the flasher. The memory brought a smile to his mouth. He had to admit he'd felt foolish standing there buck naked in front of her neighbors.

Lizabeth almost fainted when he smiled. It was the small, unguarded smile of a man laughing at himself. It was a little embarrassed and utterly charming. It almost broke her heart. He was so damn lovable! "What are you smiling about?"

"I guess I was a real bozo last night."

Lizabeth laughed. She wrapped her arms around his waist and hugged him. "You were sweet."

"Really?"

"Mmmm. I was the bozo. I overreacted."

"No, no. You were right," Matt said. "I went berserk. I lost control."

"True. You did lose control."

"I had good reason to lose control, Lizabeth. The man is a nut-case. And now he's resorting to violence."

Lizabeth rolled her eyes. "He got frustrated and threw his shoe at my window. I'd hardly call that violent. You, on the other hand, are prone to violence. You even *enjoy* violence. You keep a whole cardboard boxful of violence. And you watch hockey! You probably like boxing and wrestling too."

"So sue me. I'm a man. Men like those things."

"Not *my* men, buster!" she shouted.

"Unh!" She thunked her fist against her forehead. She was doing it again. What was wrong with her? She was unreasonable. She was making a mess of things. She took a deep breath. "Maybe we should go home."

Matt vented his exasperation on the beer can, crushing it flat. "How many homes are you talking about? Are we still married?"

"We're talking about my home . . . our home," she corrected. "And we're still married. At least until I can come up with a better story. Is that okay with you?"

"Anything's okay with me as long as I can get out of this suit."

Eight

Lizabeth dropped a cotton nightshirt over her head. She fluffed the pillows on her bed, turned down the sheet and summer comforter, and set the alarm. What she needed was a good night's sleep in her nice comfy bed, she thought. She needed space, some time to think. And she needed rest. She crawled into bed and groaned out loud as her spine relaxed and her bare legs slid between the cool sheets. The sound of swearing carried to her from down the hall. There was a loud crash and more swearing. A door opened and then slammed shut. It was Matt. Now what? What more could possibly go wrong? They had snapped at each other all through supper. After supper she had refused to go riding on his motorcycle, and he had refused to watch *Out of Africa*, saying it was a sissy movie. Now he was stomping around like a bear wearing lead boots.

Matt looked at her closed door and counted to ten. Calm yourself, he said. You know how she hates violence. You know how she hates when you lose control and go running around naked. Okay, he had that one covered. He'd put on a pair of pajama bottoms.

He knocked on the door.

"Yes?"

He sucked in a lungful of air. "I have to talk to you."

"I'm tired. Can't we talk tomorrow?"

"No. We can't talk tomorrow. We have to talk now."

"I don't want to talk now." She didn't want to talk to someone who called *Out of Africa* a sissy movie. And he'd implied her mashed potatoes were lumpy. And he'd yelled at Ferguson just because Ferguson had eaten his shoe. And more than that, she wasn't up to having him in her bedroom. She couldn't get a grip on her emotions. There was love and fear and anger all jumbled together, and she couldn't stop them from tumbling out. Ever since last night she had been saying things she regretted, and yet, she kept saying them.

He did some deep breathing, counted to ten again, tried the doorknob, and found it was locked. More deep breathing. More counting to ten. "Oh hell," he said. He gave the door a good kick and broke the lock.

Lizabeth sprang up to a sitting position, too astonished to be angry. Her eyes were wide, her mouth open. "You broke my door!"

Now that he had kicked something he was feeling much better. He was even able to speak without shouting—just barely. "That isn't all I've broken. I've also broken Jason's bed. I don't fit in a twin size."

"Have you tried the couch?"

"Ferguson's sleeping on the couch." He slapped the spare pillow into shape and turned back the sheet.

Lizabeth felt panic claw at her throat. "You're not sleeping here!"

"The hell I'm not." He rolled in beside her and gave something that was close to a growl. "I don't fit in this bed either. Every bed in this house was designed for midgets."

"I didn't hear you complaining last night."

"Last night I wasn't interested in sleeping."

"And I suppose the only thing you have on your mind tonight is sleeping?"

"You got it."

How insulting! They'd been married for less than twenty-four hours and he wanted to go to sleep. Of course, it wasn't a real marriage, but it was insulting all the same. She glared down at him. "Well, since you don't fit in this bed you might as well go somewhere else. Why don't you go kick Billy's door down and ruin his bed."

"Don't push me, Liz. I'm a man on the edge."

She gave him a long, considering look and decided to let him teeter. "Hmmm," she said, slithering down beside him.

"What's 'hmmm' supposed to mean?"

"Nothing. Just hmmmm." She shut the light off and smiled in the darkness, deciding she liked having him next to her. She liked the way his warmth cut through her nightgown. She liked listening to him breathe, liked the way he made her feel safe from whatever terrors the night might hold. Now that she had a chance to reconsider, she might even like to make love to him. " 'Night," she whispered, rustling closer as she turned her back, not so innocently snuggling her bottom into his hip.

He didn't respond. He couldn't. Not without giving himself away. He'd made a colossal mistake. He'd been hurt when she'd suggested he sleep in Jason's room. As the night wore on he'd become more and more frustrated. The bed had been the last straw, but in all honesty, if he hadn't been thrashing around in a snit, the bed would never have collapsed. Now he was next to her, and he was miserable. He'd told her he was only interested in sleeping. Yeah, he thought, and cows can fly. Every muscle in his body felt as if it were tied in knots. He was hard—everywhere. And he was supposed to sleep?

He turned toward her and put his hand to her waist, feeling the flare of her hip. She would have been pretty when she was a teenager, he decided. But as a fully grown woman she was magnificent. Her breasts were full, her nipples large and dark from nursing two children, and her lips were as soft as her breasts. He liked the way she tipped her head back and laughed deep in her throat. Honest laughter. And he liked the way she made love to him. Honest loving. His thumb stroked over the ridge of hipbone. "Lizabeth?"

She twisted in his arms until she was facing

him, her breasts brushing against his bare chest, her face inches from his.

Matt feathered his lips against her forehead when he spoke. "I think our marriage hasn't gotten off to a good start."

"I've noticed that, but I don't know how to fix it. Maybe it's unfixable." Sometimes love just isn't enough, she thought. Sometimes there were differences that couldn't be bridged. Sometimes there were personalities that couldn't adapt. Some people simply weren't meant to be married. Maybe she was one of those people. The possibility brought a new rush of sadness, and she sought solace from it in Matt's embrace. She was tired of being sad. She had spent too many sad nights with Paul. She raised her mouth to Matt, and her lips trembled when he kissed her. Lord, how she loved him. If they had only met at another time— when the boys were grown, or before they'd been born. His kisses were gentle but persistent. His hands moved under her nightshirt and the feel of his calloused palm on her bare belly pulled her away from thought. Desire warmed her, drugged her. She gave herself up to it, needing to be part of him for a little while longer.

Lizabeth woke to the aroma of coffee brewing and the smoky smell of bacon frying. It was six A.M. and responsibility lay heavy on her. So heavy she could barely open her eyes or raise her arms. She was going to have to cut Matt out of her life, and the wound was going to be unbearably painful and impossible to heal. She'd been a fool to let things go this far. She'd had some misgivings before—silly ones about tattoos and education, but when Paul left with her kids it had triggered an anxiety attack that had raised serious, legitimate questions. When you combined the serious questions with the silly misgivings it didn't seem like the relationship had much of a chance for long-term success. She was a mother. That was the bottom line. And the mothering part of her was strong. So strong there was a tendency for it to squeeze out everything else. Perhaps because all her life she'd been Mac's daughter or Paul's wife, now she couldn't keep herself from being Jason and Billy's mother. She'd make a terrible wife. She didn't know how to divide herself up so that there was some for Billy and Jason, and some for Matt, and some for Lizabeth. Matt would be neglected, she thought. In a small corner of her mind she couldn't help compare Matt to Paul and wonder if Matt would eventually find comfort in other women. Even as she thought these things, a tear trickled down her cheek, and she wasn't sure if it was for Jason or Billy or Matt or herself.

Sirens wailed in the distance, and she absently wondered if it was the police chasing down the flasher. No, she decided, the flasher wouldn't be running around at six in the morning. Anyway, there were too many sirens. She could hear the throaty blast of air horns now. Fire trucks. And they were getting closer. She got out of bed and dragged herself to Elsie's room at the front of the house. She looked out the window and watched the trucks turn onto Gainsborough. They swung wide at the corner and headed in her direction, lights flashing. She looked down the street, but saw no evidence of a fire. No smoke. No flames. No unusual activity. Two large trucks and a smaller rescue vehicle stopped in front of her house. She could feel the vibration of the engines deep in her chest, felt the lights pulsing against her nightshirt.

They were obviously lost. Someone's house was burning to the ground and the firemen were lost. Who cares, Lizabeth thought. She was depressed. She wasn't even sure she'd care if it were her house that was burning. That was when she smelled the smoke. That was when she noticed her eyes were smarting. That was when Matt opened the front door just below her and waved to the firemen. The lethargy instantly lifted and was replaced with panic. "Matt! What's going on?" she shouted.

He looked up at her. "Hi, honey. Don't worry. Everything's okay. I just burned the bacon a little." Did she believe that?

"What are these fire trucks doing here?"

"The bacon kept smoldering. And I figured better safe than sorry." He flashed her a reassuring smile.

One of the firemen rushed past Matt. He was in full protective gear, carrying a fire extinguisher. He grinned and shook his head at Matt. "Burned the bacon a little? Man, I got a look at the back of this house when we turned the corner. You barbecued your kitchen! You're in big trouble. She's gonna kick your butt all the way around the block."

Matt grinned back at him. "So, you think she'll notice the damage?"

Lizabeth raced down the stairs, struggling to get her arms into her bathrobe as she ran. She came to an abrupt halt at the kitchen. It was black. Black soot on the walls. Black soot on the ceiling. And the stove and part of the back wall were charred. Foam dripped from counters and appliances and grimy water flooded the floor.

"Nice work," one of the firemen said to Matt. "Use your garden hose?"

"Only after it spread to the outside wall."

Everyone looked at Lizabeth. She was standing perfectly still, her arms hanging limp at her sides, her shoulders slightly slumped. The silence was as thick as the foam on the stove. Finally, she spoke. "I want almond-colored appliances," she said. "Pot-scrubber dishwasher and self-cleaning oven. Butcher-block countertops. I think I'll wallpaper the walls. I always thought a small print would look nice in here."

By ten o'clock a cleaning crew arrived, followed by the electrician, and at eleven-thirty Grimm's Appliances delivered a range, dishwasher, state-of-the-art refrigerator, and microwave. Lizabeth was glad Matt was in the construction business. She would have had to wait weeks for a new toaster to be delivered.

Matt and Ferguson sat on the front porch, eating Oreos. "Guess I'm not so handy in the kitchen," Matt said to the dog. "I just never paid much attention to cooking before. No one ever cooked for me when I was a kid. Hey, don't worry about it. I got along okay. Look how big I grew." He took the top off an Oreo and gave it to Ferguson and kept the part with the icing for himself. "Sometimes my sister Mary Ann would cook, but it was mostly from cans or hamburgers. Nothing fancy like bacon." He separated another cookie. This time Ferguson got the good part. "I know what you're thinking. I lived in that town house for ten years. I should have learned how to cook bacon, but jeez, who would have thought the grease would catch fire like that?" He put a confiding arm around the dog. "Just between you and me, my mind was wandering. You got a girlfriend, Ferguson? Maybe you're too young. Well, let me tell you, women can be damn distracting. And wonderful," he added softly. He thoughtfully munched on an Oreo. "Lizabeth is special. You're a lucky dog to be living with Lizabeth."

Miller's Furniture truck pulled up at the curb, and Lizabeth came running to the front door. "What's that furniture truck doing here? Matt! You didn't buy furniture, did you?"

"It's a bed," Matt said, handing the bag of cookies over to Ferguson. "I couldn't spend another night in that little bitty bed you've got."

"You should have asked me."

"You would have said no."

"Exactly." Lizabeth flapped her arms. "I don't want a new bed. I can't afford a new bed."

"I bought the bed."

"Matt, that's very sweet of you, but I can't let you buy me a bed. I mean a bed isn't like a bag of doughnuts. Men don't just go around giving beds to women. I didn't mind you advancing me money for the appliances, because I know my insurance will cover it. But a bed! You can't give me a bed."

Andy Miller and Zak Szlagy carried a metal bed frame and a queen-size box spring into the house.

"Stop!" Lizabeth said. "I didn't order this."

"It's already paid for, lady," Andy said. "S'cuse me. This goes upstairs?"

Lizabeth followed after them. "I haven't room for another bed. What will I do with my double?"

"Don't worry about it. We'll take care of the double. Why don't you put it in this room where the bed looks broken?"

"Fine. Do it." Her mind went racing ahead. If she didn't replace the linoleum in the kitchen she could probably cover the cost of the bed with the insurance money.

"We have to talk," Lizabeth said to Matt. "You have to go."

"Go where?"

"Go home. To your home. This isn't working. Every day I fall a little bit deeper in love with you, and every day it becomes more and more obvious that it isn't going to work."

She was in love with him! Deeper in love with him every day. He thought his heart might jump right out of his chest. Unfortunately, she was mad at him. He couldn't figure out exactly why she was mad at him, but he decided to go with it. "All I did was buy a bed."

"It's me. I can't . . ." Her voice broke. She took a deep breath and squared her shoulders. "I'm not ready for marriage, and I can't let myself get pushed into something just because the neighbors saw you naked."

"Okay. I can live with that. I don't want you feeling pressured into anything as important as marriage. But I'm not leaving."

"What?" He wasn't teasing or flirting or being difficult. He looked deadly serious, and Lizabeth didn't think that was a good sign.

"I'm not leaving you alone in this house until the flasher's caught."

Lizabeth stuffed her hands on her hips. "Listen, mister, this is my house, and I'm kicking you out!"

"Oh yeah? You and who else?"

"Me and nobody else. I'm doing it all by myself. I'm . . ." Her attention was diverted by a delivery truck from Kantweiller's Department Store.

A young boy jumped from the truck and walked across the front yard. He handed Lizabeth a box and a clipboard. "Sign here, please."

"I don't get it," Lizabeth said. "Now what?" She sat down on the porch step and carefully opened the box. Inside was a slightly smaller box wrapped in white-and-silver paper, with a card taped to the top. "Omigod," she said, reading the card. "It's a wedding gift from Emma Newsome!"

Matt unwrapped the box. "Hey, it's a waffle iron. This is great. You know how to make waffles?"

Lizabeth sat on her big new bed all by herself. She had the oak chest of drawers pushed in front of her door, but so far it was unnecessary. Matt hadn't shown any interest in breaking her door down. He'd gone off to the job site shortly after the waffle iron was delivered and hadn't returned until six o'clock, when he'd arrived with bags of burgers and french fries. He'd made polite conversation and gone to work in the kitchen, pulling out the old cabinets. It was after twelve now, and the house was quiet. Lizabeth thought it felt lonely. She thought it wasn't a house that was comfortable with quiet. It needed noisy children and dogs that stole pot roasts. Even Ferguson seemed subdued today. And the flasher had moved on to greener pastures. He hadn't shown up last night, for the first time in five days. Probably because word got out that she was married.

She smoothed the new quilt and wiggled her toes. She couldn't sleep. She wasn't tired, and she was afraid if she turned the light off the sadness would overwhelm her, and she'd burst into tears. She had to keep busy. That was the clue to surviving, she'd decided. She could watch television, but the television and the VCR were downstairs, on the other side of the blocked door. She picked up the book she'd been reading. A love story. Not tonight. She got up and looked out the window. Her yard was dark and empty. She paced in the room. Okay, so suppose she wasn't locked up in her room. What would she do? For the first time in ten years she was alone with time on her hands. She needed a hobby. She used to knit when she was in college, but it no longer appealed to her. Gardening was good, but it was too dark to garden now. It was pretty much wasted effort, anyway, since Ferguson dug everything up. She cracked her knuckles and paced faster. Maybe athletics was the answer. She began to jog in place. This wasn't so bad. She'd planned to get into shape this summer anyway. She checked her clock. Five minutes. She was barely sweating. Not enough of a challenge. She needed to get out on the road. She pulled a pair of jogging shorts from her bottom drawer and three minutes later was lacing up her running shoes. She pushed the chest away from the door and carefully, quietly tiptoed down the hall. She was at the top of the stairs when she heard Matt's door open.

"Going somewhere?"

"Running."

Matt grinned at her. "Got excess energy?"

"I've decided to get into shape."

"At one o'clock in the morning?"

"One o'clock in the morning is a great time to run," Lizabeth said. "It's cooler, and you don't have to wear sunscreen, and there isn't any traffic."

"I don't think this is a good idea. There are weird people out there."

"This is a family neighborhood. I'll be perfectly safe."

Matt groaned. This was from the woman who thought the flasher was a nice guy. "Wait a minute, and I'll run with you."

"I don't want you to run with me."

Half an hour later Lizabeth's shirt was soaked through. Her hair hung in wet ringlets and her cheeks were flushed as she plodded beside Matt. "Are we almost home?"

"Three more blocks," Matt said. "You want to stop and walk a while?"

"Why aren't you tired? Why am I the only one sweating?"

"Guess I'm in better shape than you."

Lizabeth wiped her face with the sleeve of her T-shirt. "Yeah, baking cookies isn't exactly a heavy aerobic workout."

"Maybe not, but I bet it's fun."

There was something about his voice that caught her attention. "Haven't you ever baked cookies?"

"Nope. My cookies come already baked. Hey, I have a terrific idea. Maybe we could work out a talent trade. You could teach me to bake cookies, and I could help you exercise."

Lizabeth stopped running. She put her hands at her hips and bent forward, trying to catch her breath. "You'd do that?"

"I'd like to learn how to make pancakes too. I tried once, but they stuck to the pan. And mashed potatoes . . ."

"You don't know how to make mashed potatoes?" It was hard for her to believe he'd been on his own for ten years and never learned how to mash potatoes. She was beginning to understand all the fast-food bags in his bedroom.

"Learning how to cook is sort of like losing your virginity," he said. "You reach an age where it's embarrassing to ask someone to teach you how to go about it."

"I've never thought of it exactly that way, but I suppose you're right." She took a couple of deep breaths. "I think I'm ready. Let's try some more running."

They turned onto Gainsborough and Matt put a restraining hand on Lizabeth's arm, holding her back. "There's someone in the side yard of that gray Cape Cod."

"That's the Hoopers' house." Lizabeth looked in the direction of the Cape Cod just in time to see a flashlight blink on and sweep a second-story window. "Omigod."

Matt could clearly see the man. He was dressed in dark sweatpants, was wearing a paper bag mask, and was climbing up the side of the house on a ladder. Matt felt himself tense, felt his adrenaline kick in. "I'm gonna get this guy," he whispered.

He moved forward like a large cat, running noiselessly, and Lizabeth wondered where he'd learned to move with such stealth and power. He was across the street in seconds. The man was about to enter the window when he saw Matt charging. The man shrieked, jumped from the ladder, and ran. Matt chased after him, Lizabeth following.

"What's going on?" Mabel Hooper called from her bedroom window. "Who's out there?"

Lizabeth could hear the men crashing through bushes in front of her. They were running through backyards, trampling hedges of forsythia, leveling an occasional tomato plant. Dogs barked. House lights blazed up and down the street. The two men broke out into a stretch of open grass. Lizabeth saw Matt leap forward and tackle the fleeing man. She reached them just as Matt shone the flashlight in his face. "Oh dear," Lizabeth said, "it's Mr. Hooper."

"He was robbing his own house?"

Ed Hooper scrambled to his feet. "Who do you think you are anyway, Rambo?" He put his hand to his heart. "Scared me half to death. Jeez, don't you have anything better to do than run around the neighborhood in the middle of the night? Why aren't you home in bed like a normal person?"

Matt grabbed him. "What the hell were you doing climbing the ladder with a bag over your head?"

"It was my wife's idea. She took one of those magazine quizzes and only got two out of twenty points for sexual excitement. She figured it might be exciting if I pretended to be the flasher. She figured this would push her into the top ten percent."

Matt clapped his hand on Ed Hooper's shoulder. "Mr. Hooper, this is a family neighborhood. I don't think you should be playing games in your backyard. Keep it in the bedroom, okay?"

"I guess you're right," Ed Hooper said. "You need an extra grill for Saturday?"

"I feel a little silly," Matt said on the way home.

"I thought you handled that very nicely. You know, you're pretty conservative for a guy who has a tattoo and a motorcycle."

When they got back to the house a taxi was parked at the curb and the driver was unloading suitcases. Elsie and the boys stood on the sidewalk.

Jason was the first to see Lizabeth. "Mom!" he shouted. "Look at us. We're home!"

"Six hours in a taxi cab," Elsie said. "I feel like Humpty Dumpty when he fell off the wall. All the king's horses and all the king's men ain't never gonna get me back together again." She squinted at Lizabeth. "You two sure worked up a sweat. What are you doing out here?"

"Running," Lizabeth said. "Great cardiovascular exercise."

"It's two o'clock in the morning."

"No traffic this time of the night," Matt said.

Elsie grabbed her suitcase and headed for the house. "I just want to go to bed. I'm going to have a nice tall glass of cold milk and go to bed and sleep for a thousand years."

Lizabeth ran after her. "There's something I should explain to you about the kitchen."

"Tomorrow. I'm too tired to listen tonight." She hauled her suitcase through the front door and came to an abrupt halt when she saw the new refrigerator, gently defrosting in the living room. "What the devil?"

"It's only temporary," Lizabeth said. "We're remodeling."

Jason ran on ahead. "Oh man, look at this! Someone trashed the kitchen."

Billy was right behind him. "Boy, I'm glad I didn't do this. We're talking Cinder City here."

"It was a meteor," Matt said. "It came right through the window. I was standing there, minding my own business, cooking bacon, and this meteor landed on the frying pan and set the bacon on fire."

Lizabeth hugged Billy and Jason. "I'm glad to see you, but why are you home so soon?"

Elsie snorted. "Turned out Paul wanted the boys down there because they were having this big picnic to kick off his candidacy for governor. Paul thought it would look good if he had a family image. You know, Mr. Mom sort of thing."

"It was supposed to be Saturday, and it would have been boring," Jason said. "Everything Dad does is boring."

"You were only there for one day!" Lizabeth poured a glass of juice for her son. "How could everything be so boring in just one day?"

Jason giggled. "Dad said it was the longest day of his life."

"You don't seem too upset by it."

"It was kinda fun," Billy said. "First of all, Jason got air-sick and threw up on Dad in the airport, and there were all these photographers who took their picture. Then when we got to the house, someone put a sweat sock in the toilet . . ."

"It wasn't me," Jason said. "I swear it wasn't me."

"Anyway, the toilet overflowed, and there was toilet water everywhere. Dad yelled at Aunt Elsie and said she was incompetent, and Aunt Elsie told Dad what she thought he should do with the sock when he got it out of the toilet. It was great, Mom. You should have been there."

"Anything else?"

"It sort of went downhill after that," Elsie said.

Jason drank his juice and wiped his mouth on the back of his hand. "Billy and I were going to get up early and make Dad breakfast in bed, but Dad didn't have any good cereal. He didn't have Froot Loops or Cap'n Crunch or anything."

Elsie had her lips pressed tight together, trying not to laugh. "So they made him an egg. In the microwave. Just put the raw egg in there and exploded it! Lord, what a mess. I've never seen anything like it."

"I didn't know it would explode," Jason said. "I swear I didn't know it would explode."

Lizabeth looked at her younger son and raised an eyebrow. "Did you get to go swimming?"

"Yeah, but they have all these rules. You can't swim here and you can't swim there. And you have to stand still while you're waiting in line. And you can't run. They don't let you take any toys into the water. Not even a ball. And they make you practice swimming the whole time. You never get to have any fun."

Billy grinned at his brother. "It was fun when you dumped Dad in the pool!"

"Oh yeah!" Jason said. "Mom, he did the most awesome belly flop!"

"He was swimming with you?" Lizabeth asked. Didn't sound like the Paul she knew.

"No," Billy said. "He came to see how we were doing, and he had on this white suit and blue shirt with a red tie, and Jason dumped him in the water. Man, was he mad! And there were all these photographers there who took their picture."

"It was an accident," Jason said. "I slipped getting out of the pool and grabbed Dad's pants leg."

Lizabeth smiled at Jason. "I'm afraid to ask about the tennis lesson."

"The tennis lesson wasn't so bad," Elsie said. "But you probably want to get some rest before you hear about dinner."

"I can't believe he sent you home after just one day."

Elsie headed for the stairs. "Paul said he could see things weren't going to work out like he planned."

"Well, I'm sorry your vacation was cut short, but it's nice to have you back," Lizabeth said.

"We would have been home sooner," Billy told her, "but we missed the plane because Dad smashed his thumb in the car door. He had to go to the emergency room and have a hole drilled in his thumbnail. Boy, can he cuss!"

"That's when he called a cab," Jason said. "He said he didn't care what it cost, he was going to make sure we got back to Pennsylvania."

Nine

"This here's one heck of a barbecue," Elsie said to Lizabeth. "Must be a hundred people here." She rolled a hot dog over on the grill. "You spot the flasher yet?"

"No. This is harder than I thought. Half the men in the neighborhood fit his description." She wasn't so sure she wanted to identify him, anyway. He'd stopped flashing her, and he'd never really done any harm to anyone.

Matt ambled over and put his arm around Lizabeth. "Great barbecue." He took a hot dog from Elsie and stuffed it into a roll. "We've got seven different kinds of potato salad, six bowls of three-bean salad, four casseroles of baked beans, and something very strange with curly noodles that I'm afraid to eat. The desserts are even better. Brownies as far as the eye can see. Mrs. Kandemeyer made cupcakes, Joan Gaspitch made chocolate-chip cookies, and Eleanor Molnar brought a sheet cake that says 'Best Wishes to Lizabeth and Matt Hallahan.' "

Lizabeth winced. The dining room table was loaded with wedding presents. She felt like a fraud, and she knew she was a coward. "We need to tell these people we're not married."

"Not me," Matt said. "I'm not telling them. Besides, I like being married. I'm not too crazy about sleeping on the couch, but I like the rest of it. I don't have to eat breakfast by myself, and I get to play soccer with the kids after work, and you play Monopoly with me at night." He spread mustard on his hot dog and loaded it with relish.

Ferguson left his station at the grill and stalked Matt's hot dog.

Lizabeth watched a pack of kids run across the yard. "If I stopped playing Monopoly with you at night, would you go home?"

"Nope. I'm protecting you from the flasher."

"I think the flasher's retired."

"Why do you want me to go home? Elsie likes me. The kids like me. Ferguson likes me." He reached out and tenderly ran his fingertip along the line of Lizabeth's jaw. "I think you like me too."

"Oh yeah? What makes you think I like you?"

"You did my laundry yesterday."

Lizabeth shrugged. "I had nothing better to do. I got home from work early, and I thought I'd clean up the laundry room."

"Yes, but you bleached my sweat socks, and you used fabric softener on my T-shirts."

A smile spread through her before she could

catch it. He was right. She'd actually stood there yesterday, fondling his socks, wondering if they were soft enough and white enough.

"Four days ago you told me you loved me. You said every day you loved me a little bit more. Is that still true?"

Lizabeth sighed. "Yes. But that doesn't mean I want to get married. We've been all through this."

"I keep hoping one of these times I'll understand. So far it hasn't made much sense to me." He set his hot dog on a plate and helped himself to potato salad. Ferguson moved with lightning speed and grabbed the frankfurter. "That dog is going to need his stomach pumped before the day is over."

"He's just a puppy."

"He weighs a hundred and thirteen pounds."

Lizabeth was distracted by a man on the far side of the dessert table. She didn't know his name, but his face was familiar. He was one of those people you periodically run into in the supermarket or at the dry cleaner. He reminded her somewhat of Paul, with his bland, pleasant smile and calculated postures. A lawyer, she decided— probably trust. He wore new docksiders, khaki slacks, and a white button-down shirt. He was in his early thirties, she thought, and a little soft around the edges. He acknowledged Emma and Al Newsome, poured himself a glass of soda, said hello to the Hoopers, and continued to move through the crowd. The whole while he moved, his eyes kept returning to Lizabeth.

An uneasy feeling rolled in her stomach. It was the flasher. If someone had asked her how she knew, she wouldn't have been able to tell them. She simply knew. She waved and he waved back. A small, hesitant wave with just his fingertips. They stared at each other for a long, embarrassed moment. Now that she'd seen him she was dying to ask him *why.* Why would he do such a weird thing? Why had he chosen her? Why had he stood there in the rain? She should confront him, she thought, but she suddenly felt uncomfortable. He'd always seemed remote and harmless in his paper-bag mask, standing in a small circle of light on the other side of her window. Now that she saw him as a person she admitted Matt had been right. She knew nothing about this man. He was real. He had thoughts and obsessions and prob-lems. He could be crazy. He could be mean. He could be dangerous.

She instinctively moved closer to Matt. He was a safe place in a crazy world. He was the friend she could always count on. He had common sense and strong arms, and he loved her. She took a step backward, coming in contact with his big, hard body. "Oops," she said. "Sorry." And then she blushed, because she'd intentionally bumped into him.

Matt brushed his hand along the nape of Liza-beth's neck. There hadn't been any lovemaking since Elsie and the boys had returned, and he ached to touch Lizabeth. Her skin was warm and silky, her hair caressed the back of his hand, and he suddenly felt choked with desire. He didn't care about Ferguson or potato salad. He cared about Lizabeth. And he wondered about the man on the far side of the dessert table who kept staring at her. "You know that guy?"

"No."

"He waved to you."

"Mmmm. Well, that's because I waved first. I've been trying to find the flasher. Checking out everybody's wave."

"And?"

"He waves like him . . . but I don't know." It was an innocent fib, she thought. If she told Matt the man was the flasher he'd punch him in the nose, or he'd break all his bones. Maybe he'd do both.

Matt slid his arm around her waist, drawing her closer. "He's the right size. And he's the right age."

"Mmmm." Lizabeth let herself relax into him. They were at a party and they were supposed to be married. And she wanted to indulge herself, even if it was just for a moment. She'd kept him at arm's length for the past few days, but her heart wasn't in it. The truth is, she wanted Matt Hallahan like she'd never wanted anything in her life, and she was feeling downright deprived.

"Doesn't look like a flasher, though," Matt said. "He looks kind of wimpy."

Lizabeth smiled. "What does a flasher look like?"

"He looks like a crazed maniac. He's a man obsessed. He drools and his eyes get big as duck eggs and bulge out of his head."

"I don't see anyone here who fits that description."

Matt gave her a squeeze. "Another week of sleeping on your couch, and I'm going to be the most crazed maniac anyone has ever seen."

"Just what this neighborhood needs—another maniac."

He kissed the back of her neck. "So what about you? Are you feeling maniacal yet?"

"Nope. Not me."

"Liar."

Elsie came over. "Who's the wimpy yuppie behind the brownies? He keeps staring at you two."

"He's staring at Lizabeth," Matt said. "She waved to him."

"Oh yeah? He wave back? He don't look like a pervert, but then you never know. Maybe I should go have a talk with him."

A wave of new guests arrived, bringing more potato salad and brownies, and someone brought a ham. It was semi-boneless in an orange glaze, dotted with pineapple slices and maraschino cherries. It was placed on the potato salad table, and before the first piece could be sliced away, Ferguson galloped in and snatched the entire ham.

Elsie, Matt, and Lizabeth saw the whole thing. "Ferguson!" they shouted in unison.

Ferguson dashed through the crowd with the ham firmly stuffed into his mouth. He dodged Matt and sprinted past John Gaspitch. He knew where he was going. He always took the same escape route. Down Gainsborough to the Wainstock house, then through the Wainstocks' backyard to the patch of woods between Gainsborough and High Street.

"Get that dog!" Elsie shouted.

A dozen children ran after Ferguson.

Ferguson loped across the side yard, ran between two cars parked at the curb, and bolted into the street. There was the sound of screeching tires, and a yelp, and then there was silence.

"Oh God," Lizabeth whispered. She was running, without thinking. Matt was ahead of her.

She reached the road and Jason threw himself into her arms. "Mom! We were chasing Fergie, and he got hit." Tears were streaming down his face, leaving smeary tracks in little boy's grime. He buried his face in her chest and sobbed, and she looked past him to the inert form lying on the road.

"Oh Fergie," she whispered. He was just a puppy. Big and foolish and homely. And she'd loved him.

Children sought out parents. Everyone stood in hushed knots, waiting.

Matt and Billy were bent over the dog. Billy's voice wobbled. "He isn't going to die, is he?" he asked.

The dog was unconscious. Blood was clotted on his hind leg. Matt stroked the dog's shoulder. Damn stupid dog, he thought. More trouble than he was worth. Stealing food, ruining soccer balls. "Jeez, Ferguson," he said, "why did you have to run off with the ham?" He swallowed back the emotion clogging his throat and burning behind his eyes.

Billy huddled closer to Matt and repeated his question. "He isn't going to die, is he?"

Matt took a deep breath and pushed the possibility of death away. "Are you kidding? Ferguson's too ornery to die. Hell, this dog is strong. He can eat a whole pot roast. We're going to take him to the vet. You stay here and keep him quiet while I go get the truck." He found Lizabeth standing on the curb. "Get a blanket. We're taking Ferguson to the vet."

Fifteen minutes later, Matt, Lizabeth, Jason, and Billy stood in the waiting room of the Parkway Veterinary Clinic and watched the doors close behind Ferguson.

"They'll take good care of him," Matt said, bolstering himself as much as anyone else.

Jason held tight to his hand. "He looks awful hurt."

Matt took a seat and lifted Jason onto his lap. "We're going to wait right here until the vet's done fixing Fergie up. We're not going to leave until we're sure he's okay. Does that make you feel better?"

Jason nodded and leaned back in Matt's arms. His face was swollen and blotchy from crying, and his breath was coming in hiccups. "Dumb dog," he said. "Nothing but trouble."

Matt smiled, because it echoed his earlier thoughts. "Yup. Fergie's dumb all right. But we all love him, don't we?"

Billy sat between Matt and Lizabeth. His eyes were large and solemn. His hands gripped the sides of his seat. "Do you love Fergie?" he asked Matt.

"Yeah."

"Did you have a dog when you were a kid?"

"No. I always wanted one, but my father wouldn't allow it."

Billy looked at Matt with increased interest. "Really? My dad wouldn't allow us to have a dog either. What about your mom? Did she want a dog?"

Matt didn't answer immediately. "I didn't have a mother for a large part of my childhood," he finally said. "She died when I was seven years old."

"Didn't your dad get married again? Who took care of you?"

"My sister Mary Ann took care of me. And then when I was old enough I took care of myself."

Jason sat up straighter so he could look at Matt. His curiosity was aroused. "Did your dad take care of you too?"

"No. I hardly ever saw my dad."

"Just like us!" Jason said. "Was your dad rich like our dad?"

"My dad was a coal miner. We lived in a small wooden house on the side of a hill, surrounded by other small houses." It was hot in the summer and cold in the winter, and in all the years he lived there he couldn't ever remember the house getting painted, inside or out. He didn't tell that part to Jason. And he didn't tell him about the days when they had to beg a neighbor for food because his father had spent the food money on liquor. "I had two sisters and four brothers," Matt said. "Everyone called us the Hallahan Herd." Matt smiled. He hadn't thought about the Hallahan Herd in a long time. Usually he avoided talking about his childhood, but it wasn't painful to tell Jason and Billy. They took it on an entirely different level. It was ancient history, anecdotal, fascinating. There was no pity, no judgment passed, no scorn.

"I've never seen a coal mine," Jason said. "Is it scary?"

"Sometimes. It's a dangerous place to work." Two of his brothers were still working in the mine. Both had lung problems. One was an alcoholic, like his dad. His sisters had married miners. Lucy was already a widow. He set that part of his history aside for another time. "I didn't want to work in the mines," Matt told the boys. "There wasn't enough money for me to go to college, so I joined the Navy as soon as I graduated from high school. When I got out of the Navy I wanted a job where I would always be outdoors, so I decided to build houses."

He looked at Lizabeth and found she was as fascinated as her children.

It wasn't the coal-miner stories that fascinated Lizabeth. It was Matt's willingness to dip into a painful past to take everyone's mind off Ferguson. She remembered the unopened envelope from his father and finally understood some of Matt's bitterness. He'd been neglected as a child, and now he was only remembered for the money he sent home.

Jason rubbed his eyes. "I'm thirsty. I got empty from crying."

"There's a convenience store down the street," Matt said. "I could go get some sodas."

Jason squirmed off Matt's lap. "Can I go with you?"

"You bet. I'll tell you about the time I was a boxer."

"Wow!" Jason said. "You were a boxer? That's so radical."

Matt shook his head. "I was the worst boxer ever. I didn't like hitting people, and I *hated* when people hit me. One time I had this match with Killer Gruzinsky from Jersey City . . ."

Billy slid off his seat. "Can I go too? I want to hear about Killer Gruzinsky."

They all looked at Lizabeth. "You guys go ahead," she said. "I'll stay here and wait for news about Fergie." Well, will you look at that, she thought. There go the men in my life. It was a brand-new experience. She couldn't ever remember seeing Paul go off hand in hand with his sons. It was such a simple thing—an excursion to buy sodas. She watched them walk away and was struck by a mind-boggling idea. Matt was carving the pie up for her. He was taking over some of the responsibility of parenthood and leaving her with time for herself. He loves me, she thought. He loves my children. He even loves my dog. Maybe their educational differences had evened out. She had a college degree, and he'd been a boxer. It was all life experience, she told herself. She slumped down in her seat and giggled. He'd been a boxer! "Lizabeth," she said, "your life is getting curiouser and curiouser."

She was waiting in the parking lot when they came back with their sodas. "Ferguson is okay," Lizabeth said. "He has a broken leg, but the vet thinks he's going to be fine. He's going to stay here tonight. Unless there are complications we can come pick him up in the morning."

"Is he gonna have a cast on his leg?" Billy wanted to know.

"Yup. I went back to see him, and he has a big white cast on his hind leg. You guys can be the first to sign it tomorrow."

The yard was clean and the house was quiet when they got home. Elsie met them at the door.

"He's all right," Lizabeth said. "Broken leg. He's spending the night at the vet."

Elsie wiped her eyes with a tissue. "Dang dog is a pain in the behind."

Lizabeth slipped an arm around Elsie's waist and hugged her. "I think when the cast comes off we'll take Ferguson to obedience school. Maybe when I can save up some money I'll have part of the yard fenced."

Elsie led the way into the kitchen. "I imagine you folks could use some supper. I have some cold fried chicken and lots of leftover salad." She pulled dishes from the refrigerator. "The party broke up right after Ferguson got hit. Folks were real nice." She turned with a dish of pickles in her hand. "You know, I talked to that young man. The one you told Matt waved like the flasher."

Lizabeth gave Elsie her full attention. "Yes?"

"I didn't mention nothing about flashing to him. I was just talking to him about things, and turns out he knows Paul."

Lizabeth felt herself go numb. "What else did he say?"

"Nothing else. We didn't talk too long. He was telling me how he lives in them new town houses on Center Street."

"You remember his name?"

"Richard. I don't remember the last part."

Lizabeth took a plate and piled fried chicken on it. She added a glob of potato salad, a glob of three-bean salad, and four brownies. She stuck a fork into it and handed it to Matt. "Here. You can eat your supper in the car."

"Where are we going?"

"I'm going to talk to this Richard person. You're going with me to make sure I don't kill him."

Lizabeth went to the garage and unlocked the doors. A hundred years ago the garage had been a carriage house. No one had bothered to modernize it. It still had a dirt floor and hayloft and was more charming than functional. Lizabeth opened one of the big double doors while Matt stood to the side with his plate of food.

"Son of a gun, there's a car in here! I've never seen you drive a car. I didn't think you owned one."

"I don't drive it any more than I have to. Poor thing's seen better days."

Matt walked into the cool, dusty interior of the carriage house and tried not to look too horrified at the little foreign import. It was orange, and to say it had seen better days was an understatement. It was missing both bumpers and a back fender. Rust was rampant, the antenna had been snapped off, and it had a yellow diagonal sign in the back window that said, "Fairy on Board." Matt added "renovate carriage house" and "buy Lizabeth new car" to the checklist he'd been carrying in his head. "Lizabeth, why don't you just drive my truck?"

"It's too big." She yanked the rusted door open and slid behind the wheel. "Besides, my car needs some exercise." She patted the seat next to her. "Don't worry. It's safe. It's passed inspection and everything."

Matt looked at the inspection sticker on the windshield. "Lizzy, this inspection sticker is from Virginia, and it expired three years ago."

"Well, for goodness' sake, I hardly ever drive the car. What could happen to it in three years?" She backed out of the driveway, undaunted by the clatter of knocking valves. She slowed at the corner and the car gave a death-throes shudder, but continued to run.

Matt smiled and ate his chicken. Lizabeth was a Hawkins through and through. He imagined if the car had the audacity to die Lizabeth would go out and give it a kick and get it to start one more time.

Lizabeth pulled into a pipe stem at the end of Center Street and parked in the small lot. It was a new subdivision of expensive brick town houses. Yards were professionally maintained, windows were clothed in custom drapes, doors were heavy oak with leaded windows and classy brass handles.

"How are we going to find him?" Matt asked. "We don't know his house number or his last name. There must be twenty houses here."

"Most of these houses have names written on the door knockers. If I can't find him that way I'll ask someone. If no one knows him I'll go door-to-door until I find him."

"You're really serious about this."

Lizabeth's mouth was compressed into a thin line. "Darn right I'm serious. Paul had something to do with this. I can feel it in my bones."

Matt left his plate in the car and followed after Lizabeth.

She stopped at the fifth house. "Here's a possibility—R. Hastings." She rapped the brass door knocker and chewed on her lower lip while she waited.

Richard Hastings opened the door and gave a surprised gasp when he saw Lizabeth. His eyes grew wide and frightened when he saw Matt. He tried to slam the door shut, but Matt had his foot rammed against it.

Matt wrapped his hand around Hastings' arm and pulled him outdoors. "Maybe you should step out here before the wind blows the door shut again," Matt said.

Hastings flinched. "You aren't going to hit me, are you?"

"Hell no," Matt said. "I'm here to protect you." He jerked a thumb at Lizabeth. "*She's* here to hit you."

Richard Hastings looked indignant. "Why would she want to hit me? I was the one who had to stand in her backyard, feeling like a damn fool with no clothes on."

Lizabeth narrowed her eyes. "What are you talking about?"

Hastings gave Matt a sympathetic shake of the head. "Just between you and me, I think you've got a hard road ahead of you with all this exhibitionist stuff. I have to tell you, I wasn't all that unhappy when I heard she was married. Man, I was chased by cops and dogs, and then there was that crazy old lady in the Cadillac. And the mosquito bites are the worst."

"Maybe you should fill us in on this 'exhibitionist' stuff. Where'd you get the idea for the Yuppie Flasher?" Matt asked.

"From Paul, of course. I met him at a law conference in Richmond. He told me all about Lizabeth, and how she was looking for a husband, but she had this kinky thing about exhibitionists. I tried to meet her through normal channels. I called and introduced myself, but she wasn't interested. I purposely ran into her in the supermarket a couple times, but she froze me out. So I decided to give it one last shot and try the Yuppie Flasher."

"I'm going to kill him," Lizabeth said. "I'm going to hunt Paul down and break every bone in his body."

"Tsk, tsk, tsk," Matt said. "That's so violent."

"No hard feelings," Richard Hastings said to Matt. "I know she's due to inherit a ton of money, but hell, you're gonna need it to make bail."

"Wait a minute," Matt said. "What about Angie Kuchta? Why did you flash her?"

Hastings grimaced. "That's what happens when you try to do a good deed. I was walking through the yards to get to Lizabeth's house, and I looked up, and there was this woman getting undressed in front of her window. She wasn't doing it on purpose. She just hadn't thought to close her curtains. So I threw a stone up at her to tell her to close her curtains. That's a nice neighborhood, but you never know when some weirdo is skulking around."

Matt and Lizabeth exchanged glances.

"Anyway, this woman takes one look at me and starts screaming!"

"Come on, cowboy," Matt said to Lizabeth. "I think it's time to head the wagon train for home."

Lizabeth got into the orange car. "I suppose this is as close as Paul gets to a sense of humor."

It was a quiet ride home. Lizabeth pulled into the dusky interior of the carriage house, cut the engine, and sat studying the steering wheel, feeling swallowed up by the sudden silence. She was physically and mentally exhausted, but she felt at peace. It was as if she'd tossed a box of puzzle pieces into the air and when the pieces had fallen to the ground they'd all fit together.

Matt had his knees pressed against the dashboard. "Lizabeth, I don't fit in this car."

Lizabeth smiled. "I suppose that means you're going to buy me a new one."

Matt laughed. "I suppose it does. I hope I get more use out of it than the bed."

"I've been meaning to talk to you about the bed."

Matt didn't want to hear it. She was going to tell him to take it back, or she was going to tell him she'd pay for it by taking in laundry or something equally ridiculous. Things weren't going well for him. First Elsie came home early and now they'd settled the problem of the flasher. Staying at Lizabeth's house to protect her from the flasher had been a pretty flimsy excuse, but now he was left with nothing. He was going to have to move out. His sweat socks would get gray again. He'd be lonely at night, and lonely in the morning, and feverish with frustration all day at work. Man, life was the pits. He'd trade with Ferguson any day of the week. So Ferguson had a broken leg. Big deal. Ferguson got to live with Lizabeth. "Okay, what about the bed?"

"It's too big. I don't fit in it all by myself."

"Uh-huh."

"And another thing. It doesn't look right for people who are married to sleep apart. I mean, what will the kids think? They'll think Mom and Dad don't like each other."

"That's true. I've always said that. What are we talking about?"

Lizabeth rolled her eyes. Men were so dense. "We're talking about us."

"But we're not really married," Matt said.

"I know, and I think that's something we should correct as soon as possible."

It took a full minute for the realization to hit home. She wanted to marry him! He felt giddy with relief and happiness.

Matt pinned her against the inside of the car door. "Couldn't stand it any longer, huh?" He nuzzled her neck and kissed her just below her earlobe. "What was it that finally pushed you over the edge? Was it my washed-out jeans? The ones with the hole in the knee?" He slid the strap to her sundress off her shoulder and kissed her collarbone. "Maybe it was the way I handled the kitchen fire. So masterfully." The sundress slid lower, exposing her breast. Matt drew a line around the sensitive tip with his finger, causing Lizabeth to shiver. "Ah, Lizabeth," he whispered. "How I've missed you."

She wrapped her arms around his neck and opened her mouth to him, arching in pleasure when his hand took possession of her breast. There would always be time for Matt, she thought. When their days were insanely busy there would still be the night. There would always be the night. And there would be an occasional dalliance in the garage. "Maybe you should lock the garage doors," Lizabeth said. "I hate being interrupted."

Matt levered himself out of the import. "What a hussy!"

She was in a suggestive position on the trunk when he returned. "Do you think this is undignified for a mother?"

He pulled her panties down. "I think this is perfect for a mother."

Epilogue

Lizabeth put Elsie's suitcase in the backseat of the Cadillac and hugged her aunt. "Are you sure you won't stay? Matt said he'd turn the carriage house into an apartment for you."

"That's nice of him, but I just came for the summer, and the summer is over. Now that the pervert problem is solved there isn't much excitement here. No bingo games. And you don't have any old men. My love life has gone down the toilet. I need to go where there's more action."

Ferguson impatiently sat on the front porch, his leg still encased in the plaster cast. He flopped onto his side with a clunk of the cast and watched with detached interest as Elsie drove away. At an earlier time he might have chased her car or chomped into her suitcase, but today he was reduced to the role of spectator. His ears pricked up and his tail thumped against the wood floor when Lizabeth turned his way.

She sat down with a sigh and draped an arm around the dog. Across the street the sun was setting behind the Newsomes' TV antenna. "What a great sunset," Lizabeth said to Ferguson. "We're lucky we get to sit here and watch it."

Ferguson made a desperate sound and pushed against her until she scratched his neck. Next week the cast would come off, and Lizabeth guessed Ferguson would be as obnoxious as ever. She was almost looking forward to it.

She twisted the gold band on her finger and felt a rush of happiness. Her life was perfect. She amended that to *almost* perfect. There was still the motorcycle. It was a terrific motorcycle—if you liked motorcycles. After all, it was a hog. "I'm never going to be a motorcycle person," she admitted to Ferguson. "We aren't going to tell that to Matt, because he dearly loves the blasted thing." She anxiously looked up the street. Matt and Billy had taken the Harley out two hours ago. They weren't usually gone this long, and she was worried. She always worried when Matt was out on the Harley. He'd told her how safe it was and explained about quality construction, but she worried all the same.

The screen door slammed and Jason ran out and flopped down next to Ferguson. "This is so-o-o-o boring. Nobody can play, and there's nothing on television. How come Billy got to go out on the Harley and I didn't?"

"Because you went out yesterday."

"It isn't fair."

Lizabeth's eyes were drawn back to the street. They'd been gone too long. Something was wrong. Usually she heard the Harley rumbling around the neighborhood. You could hear it a mile away. Today everything was quiet. "Why don't you get a book," Lizabeth said to Jason. "We'll read a story together."

He looked past her, down the street, and his eyes got wide. "Wow!" he said. "Look at this! This is awesome!" He scrambled to his feet and took off across the lawn.

Lizabeth followed. There was a car pulling into her driveway. A brand-new, shiny, black-and-burgundy jeep-type thing that had *4x4* written in big black letters across its flank. It sat high on slightly oversize tires and had bug-eye spotlights attached to the roof. There was a hitch attached to the jeep thing, and attached to the hitch was a boat. A big, glistening white boat. Matt and Billy jumped out of the burgundy jeep.

"What do you think?" Matt asked. He wiped at a smudge on the boat with his shirttail. "It's a beauty, isn't it?"

Lizabeth had a hard time finding her voice. "What happened to the Harley?"

"I traded it in. Billy and I were cruising down the highway and we passed this boat place, and I said to myself, That's what we need! We need a boat! We can all go out together on a boat. Nobody has to get left at home anymore."

"Can we afford a boat?"

"I had some money set aside for the house I was always going to build myself. I thought I'd get a new toy instead, and we'll put the rest in a trust fund for college expenses."

Lizabeth almost passed out from relief. No more motorcycle. No more speeding around. "What about the car? It looks like a new car, too."

"I needed it to pull the boat."

"Of course."

Jason had climbed into the boat and was sitting in the captain's chair behind the wheel. "This is so cool. Can we take it out now? Can we take it down to the river?"

"You bet," Matt said. "We're going to take your mother for a spin. Wait'll you see what this honey can do, Lizabeth. It's a sportcruiser. Thirty feet of sleek balsa wood and fiberglass."

"It's got a deep V-hull design," Billy said. "That's for racing. This hummer can move, Mom!"

"Three hundred horsepower inboard marine motor," Matt told her. "The next best thing to good sex," he whispered in her ear.

THE EDITOR'S CORNER

May is a special month here at LOVESWEPT. It's our anniversary month! We began publishing LOVESWEPTs in May 1983, and with your encouragement and support we've been at it ever since. One of the hallmarks of the LOVESWEPT line has always been our focus on our authors. The six authors whose books you can look forward to next month represent what we feel is the true strength of our line—a blend of your favorite tried-and-true authors along with several talented newcomers. The books these wonderful writers have penned just for you are as unique and different as the ladies themselves.

Helen Mittermeyer leads off the month with the second book in her *Men of Ice* trilogy, **BLACK FROST**, LOVESWEPT #396. Helen's legions of fans often remark on the intensity of emotion between her characters and the heightened sense of drama in her novels. She won't disappoint you at all with **BLACK FROST**! Hero Bear Kenmore, a race-car driver with nerves of steel, gets the thrill of his life when he meets heroine Kip Noble. Bear has never met a woman whose courage and daring equals his own, but Kip is his match in every way. For Kip, falling in love with Bear is like jumping into an inferno. She's irrevocably drawn to him yet has to struggle to keep her independence. Helen has once again created characters who barely keep from spontaneously combusting when they're together. Helen's "men of ice" are anything but!

Jan Hudson's latest treat is **STEP INTO MY PARLOR**, LOVESWEPT #397. With three previous books to her credit, this sassy Texas lady has captured your attention and doesn't plan to let it go! She brings characters to life who are true to themselves in every way and as straightforward as Jan herself. You'll enjoy the ride as her unabashedly virile hero, Spider Webb, falls hard for lovely socialite Anne Foxworth Jennings. Anne is out of cash and nearly out of hope when she meets the seductive pirate, Spider. He almost makes her forget she has to stay one step ahead of the man who'd threatened her life. But in Spider's arms she's spellbound, left breathless with yearning. Caught in his tender web, Anne discovers that she no longer fears for her life because Spider has captured her soul. **STEP INTO MY PARLOR** will grab you from page one!

Joan Elliott Pickart's **WHISPERED WISHES**, LOVESWEPT

(continued)

#398, tells the love story of Amnity Ames and Tander Ellis. You may remember Tander as the sexy computer expert friend of the hero from **MIXED SIGNALS**, #386. Joan just had to give Tander his due, and he falls for Amnity like a rock! Can you imagine a gorgeous hunk walking into a crafts store and telling the saleswoman he's decided to take up needlepoint! Tander does just that and Amnity never suspects he's got ulterior motives—she's too busy trying to catch her breath. Joan's characters always testify to the fact that there is a magical thing called love at first sight. Her books help renew your spirit and gladden your heart. You won't be able to resist feeling an emotional tug when Amnity whispers her wishes to Tander. Enjoy this special story!

One of the newcomers to LOVESWEPT is Terry Lawrence—an author we think has an exciting future ahead of her. You may have read Terry's first LOVESWEPT, **WHERE THERE'S SMOKE, THERE'S FIRE,** which was published in the fall of 1988. Since then, Terry has been hard at work and next month her second book for us hits the shelves, **THE OUTSIDER,** LOVESWEPT #399. Both the hero and the heroine of this sensually charged romance know what it's like to be outsiders, and in each other's arms they discover what it feels like to belong. When Joe Bond catches Susannah Moran switching dice in the casino he manages in his Ottawa Indian community, he has to admit the lady is good—and temptingly beautiful. Just doing her job investigating the casino's practices, Susannah has to admit she's never been caught so fast and never by a man who set off alarms all over her body! These two special people don't find it easy to bridge the differences between their cultures. But what does come easily is the overwhelming need and desire they feel for each other. Terry will surely win loads of new readers with this tender, evocatively written love story. You'll want to count yourself among them!

We published Patt Bucheister's very first LOVESWEPT, **NIGHT AND DAY,** back in early 1986, and what a smash debut it was! Now, many books and many fans later, Patt presents you with another delicious delight, **THE ROGUE,** LOVESWEPT #400. A warm and generous lady with a sunny disposition, Patt naturally creates such a heroine in Meredith Claryon. When Meredith receives a strange phone call one night from a man demanding she answer his ques-

(continued)

tions, Meredith handles the situation with her usual grace and aplomb. Paul Rouchett is so intrigued by the lady he's never met that he decides he has no choice but to convince her to team up with him to find the embezzler who'd robbed his nightclub and run off with her sister. And what a team they make! The tart-tongued nurse and the owner of the Rogue's Den are an unbeatable duo—but discovering that for themselves leads them on a merry, romantic chase. Patt's strong belief in love and romance couldn't come across better than in this well-crafted book.

Have you every wondered exactly what makes a guy a good ol' boy? Having lived my entire life north of the Mason-Dixon line, I can tell you I have! But after reading **LOVIN' A GOOD OL' BOY** by Mary Kay McComas, LOVESWEPT #401, I wonder no more. Hero Buck LaSalle is a good ol' boy in the flesh, and when Yankee Anne Hunnicut hits town in her high heels and designer suits, Buck leaves no doubt in her mind about the term. He has the sexiest smile she's ever seen and too much charm for his own good, and although he's none too pleased about why she's there, he shows her in more ways than she ever imagined how much he wants her to stay. With her inimitable style, Mary Kay will have you giggling or sighing with pleasure or shedding a tear—probably all three—before you finish this sure-to-please romance. You'll long for a good ol' boy of your own.

Since we like to set the books in our anniversary month apart, we're going to surprise you with our cover design next month. But you're used to surprises from us, right? It makes life more interesting—and fun!

All best wishes.

Sincerely,

Susann Brailey

Susann Brailey
Editor
LOVESWEPT
Bantam Books
666 Fifth Avenue
New York, NY 10103

FAN OF THE MONTH

Jane Calleja

It was the colorful cover which prompted me to buy my first LOVESWEPT. I was already an avid reader of romance books then, but the unique stories and interesting characters in the LOVESWEPTs brought new meaning to romance for me.

New issues arrived here in the Philippines each month featuring original and delightful plots. I fell in love with the heroes and heroines of Barbara Boswell, Iris Johansen, Fayrene Preston, Joan Elliott Pickart, Kay Hooper, and Sandra Brown. The authors were able to capture everyday human emotions and make their characters come alive. I would like to thank these writers for answering my letters despite their hectic schedules.

My wish is to be able to join the ranks of the LOVESWEPT authors in the future. Right now I am nineteen years old and a third-year college student. I love reading LOVESWEPTs so much that I read the same books over and over again. In fact, I've read **FOR THE LOVE OF SAMI** by Fayrene Preston more than ten times, and I plan to read it again soon. Once I start to read, I really lose track of time and place. My family just watches me queerly if I suddenly giggle or cry in the middle of reading a book. That's how vivid LOVESWEPTs are! You can't help but feel what the characters are feeling.

I was surprised, but honored and delighted to be chosen a Fan of the Month. Thank you!

60 Minutes to a Better, More Beautiful You!

Now it's easier than ever to awaken your sensuality, stay slim forever—even make yourself irresistible. With Bantam's bestselling subliminal audio tapes, you're only 60 minutes away from a better, more beautiful you!

__ 45004-2	**Slim Forever**	$8.95
__ 45112-X	**Awaken Your Sensuality**	$7.95
__ 45081-6	**You're Irresistible**	$7.95
__ 45035-2	**Stop Smoking Forever**	$8.95
__ 45130-8	**Develop Your Intuition**	$7.95
__ 45022-0	**Positively Change Your Life**	$8.95
__ 45154-5	**Get What You Want**	$7.95
__ 45041-7	**Stress Free Forever**	$7.95
__ 45106-5	**Get a Good Night's Sleep**	$7.95
__ 45094-8	**Improve Your Concentration**	$7.95
__ 45172-3	**Develop A Perfect Memory**	$8.95

THE DELANEY DYNASTY

THE SHAMROCK TRINITY

☐	21975 RAFE, THE MAVERICK *by Kay Hooper*	$2.95
☐	21976 YORK, THE RENEGADE *by Iris Johansen*	$2.95
☐	21977 BURKE, THE KINGPIN *by Fayrene Preston*	$2.95

THE DELANEYS OF KILLAROO

☐	21872 ADELAIDE, THE ENCHANTRESS *by Kay Hooper*	$2.75
☐	21873 MATILDA, THE ADVENTURESS *by Iris Johansen*	$2.75
☐	21874 SYDNEY, THE TEMPTRESS *by Fayrene Preston*	$2.75

THE DELANEYS: *The Untamed Years*

☐	21899 GOLDEN FLAMES *by Kay Hooper*	$3.50
☐	21898 WILD SILVER *by Iris Johansen*	$3.50
☐	21897 COPPER FIRE *by Fayrene Preston*	$3.50

THE DELANEYS II

☐	21978 SATIN ICE *by Iris Johansen*	$3.50
☐	21979 SILKEN THUNDER *by Fayrene Preston*	$3.50
☐	21980 VELVET LIGHTNING *by Kay Hooper*	$3.50